POWERLESS

STEEL DEMONS MC BOOK TWO

CRYSTAL ASH

SDMC series playlist

All American Nightmare - Hinder
Notorious - Adelitas Way
Hail to the King - Avenged Sevenfold
Joan of Arc - In This Moment
Radioactive - Imagine Dragons
Bad Company - Five Finger Death Punch
Love Me to Death - No Resolve
(Don't Fear) The Reaper - HIM
David - Noah Gunderson
Blue on Black - Five Finger Death Punch
Machine Gun Blues - Social Distortion
Wanted Dead or Alive - Chris Daughtry
I Get Off - Halestorm
You Shook Me All Night Long - AC/DC
Nobody Praying for Me - Seether
Loyal to No One - Dropkick Murpheys
Be Free   King Dude & Chelsea Wolfe
Raise Hell - Dorothy
Coming Home - Skylar Grey

Click here to listen on Spotify!

Prologue

JANDRO

THREE YEARS PRE-COLLAPSE

The coffee stopped kicking in six hours ago, but I choked down the bitter liquid anyway. It was the only thing that kept me going on this sixteen-hour shift. My fourth double-shift this week.

I winced at the sound of Sergeant Crodick's baton clanging on the inmates' metal doors. What an asshole. Guards, inmates, and even other supervisors hated that guy. Sure, this was the mental health building, where most inmates paced, rocked, scratched the walls, and talked to themselves at all hours of the night. But some of them were trying to sleep, too, goddamnit.

That smug asshole knocked his baton on every. Single. Cell door.

Whoever was awake became agitated, slamming their palms on the doors and yelling through the small plexiglass window. That alerted anyone who'd been sleeping, jolted awake by the initial clang and now disoriented by all the commotion.

Crodick chuckled as he returned back to the office. My grim expression apparently amused him even more.

"There ya go, rookie." He sat down in the chair and propped his feet up on the desk. "Get busy and settle the nut jobs down." With a lace of his fingers over his belly, he leaned his head back and closed his eyes. It didn't even take a minute for him to start snoring.

"Asshole," I grumbled, tossing my paper coffee cup into the trash can.

So much for a relaxing rest of the shift. I had a sinking feeling he'd call me for overtime again tomorrow. The supervisors always begged and pleaded and harassed the new guards to stay. Turnover was high at these government facilities while pay and benefits were laughably nonexistent. Only the old-timers could sit back and collect a decent check. Their wages had been negotiated back when labor unions still had power. Nowadays the newcomers did all the dirty work for basically slave wages.

We all knew the world was going to hell in a handbasket, it was just a matter of when. The twenty-year veterans who still had some value in their retirement accounts were just waiting for the right moment to cash out. They watched the slimy politicians pandering for votes and threw their support behind the most outlandish claims and emptiest promises—usually something to protect the dwindling assets they spent a lifetime building.

My generation? Oh, we were fucked. And no one gave a shit.

My footsteps were heavy as I walked out onto the floor, pulling my baton from the loop in my belt. Some inmates went quiet at just the sight of me holding it.

A sigh deflated my chest, the baton heavy in my hand. This wasn't me. I got no pleasure out of yelling at people in cages, many of whom didn't even know what was going on. All I wanted to do was fix motorcycles and bring a girl home once in a while. I didn't get paid enough to find any joy in scaring people.

Crodick was already asleep, so why did it matter if the inmates kept yelling and hitting the doors? If I got fired for insubordination, good fucking riddance.

I walked the floor like a zombie, then ascended the stairs to the upper tier. I looked straight in front of me, but my eyes didn't focus on anything. *Damn, my feet and back hurt like a bitch.* At twenty-one years old, this job already had me aching like an old man. Fuck, I just wanted to go home.

Just like on the floor, the inmates on the upper tier went quiet at the sight of me. No yelling or baton-banging necessary. Some of them were probably spooked by when I first got hired and did some baton-swinging to prove myself. Now a whole two months later, I was so fucking over it.

One cell at the end didn't quiet down like the rest. I paused in front of the door to the sound of incoherent mumbling, followed by guttural, tortured screaming.

"Hey," I knocked my baton on the door twice. "Calm down in there and go to sleep."

I heard a series of thumping sounds, like a body being thrown against the walls, then whimpering and more screams.

"Hey!" I knocked harder on the door. "I said calm the fuck down and go to sleep!"

"I can't!"

The answer startled me. Not that it was unusual for inmates to talk to us, but amid all the mumbling and screaming, those two words sounded strangely coherent.

I pulled my flashlight from my belt, clicked it on and shined it through the square window.

A pale, skinny kid shielded his eyes from where he sat against the wall. He wore the white inmate-issued pants but had taken his shirt off, as many of the male inmates did to sleep.

"Jesus fuck," I swore, lowering the light from his face to his torso.

He was covered in scar tissue. Burns, cuts, scrapes and everything imaginable crisscrossed over his thin, malnourished body. It hardly looked like he had any unmarked skin at all.

When he lowered his hands from his eyes, I saw more scarring on one side of his face. A wicked slash cut through one eye, the iris of which looked almost completely white. His other eye was dark brown, almost black like the hair buzzed close to his scalp.

"You don't have to sleep, just quit fucking scream-ing," I told him, making sure to add a hard edge to my voice.

"I'm trying!" His brow pinched tight with despair. I

could now see the tear tracks on the kid's face, who looked no older than me.

I should have walked off right then but something pulled at me to stay with him. Most of our inmates went through some kind of trauma, whether before or after coming to our facility, but I never saw anyone so broken down as this kid. Even more unusual, he seemed sane now that he wasn't screaming his head off.

I sank to the floor, getting eye-level with the small foodport slot in his door and unlocked it. *Fuck. Maybe I'm the crazy one*, I thought as I slid it open.

"Hey, come here," I said through the slot. "Tell me what's going on with you."

"No! You're going to pepper-spray me again."

Shit. When was that, yesterday? Last week? All the long shifts had blurred together so much, I forgot Crodick and his asshole buddy had coaxed inmates to look through the foodport and sprayed them for fun.

"That wasn't me," I answered. "Look, I'm a new guy. I'm not even supposed to be talking to you. But you don't seem all that crazy and I'd rather level with you than yell at you. So what's wrong?"

He didn't come closer to the door, but his shaking voice floated from across the cell.

"I'm not crazy. I just get bad nightmares when I sleep. Sometimes they stay with me as I wake up. I don't *want* to wake up screaming but I can't help it. I've been trying to stay awake but when I nod off..."

"Okay. Have they given you meds?"

"All the nurses are female! I don't take anything from women. No, never again. No, no, no."

Hmm, maybe he was a little nuttier than I thought. But on a second glance at his scarred up body, maybe not. Either way, I couldn't blame him for being distrustful.

"Okay," I repeated. "Would you accept meds if they came from a man?"

He hesitated before answering. "If they work. And if no one hits me." A soft sob echoed against the concrete walls of his cell. "I just want it to stop."

I leaned my head and shoulder against the door with a sigh. I had no power to help him. Any requests to make inmates more comfortable would be met with suspicion and scrutiny. And I wouldn't put it past Crodick and his crew to double-down on harassing this kid just because I was trying to do something nice for him.

My head lifted off the door with a start, remembering something about Crodick that I could use. *No, I* thought. *You will get tossed out of this job so fast and maybe even arrested.*

The next thought came just as quickly, spurring my tired feet to get under me. *Fuck it. You're already done with this place.*

"I'll be right back," I told the kid, leaving the food-port open as I headed for the stairs.

This was stupid, bordering on dangerous. But the world was ending and I ran out of fucks to give.

Crodick remained in the same position I left him in —hands on his belly, head leaned back, mouth open and snoring.

I came up next to him as silently as I could, then

held my breath as I slowly pulled open the file drawer just below his feet. He snorted once but didn't wake up. Only a few seconds of rummaging produced what I needed—his hidden flask of whiskey.

"When you win your first fight with an inmate, you can have a shot," he taunted me when I first got hired as he poured a generous amount into his coffee.

"Why would I fight one of them?" I had asked. "We're supposed to treat them humanely, right?"

He had doubled over laughing as if that was the funniest joke he ever heard. The memory followed me like a ghost as I left the office with the small bottle, taking it back to the door with the open foodport.

When I kneeled in front of the slot, one pale, scarred white eye and one brown eye peered at me through the opening.

"Here," I said, shoving the flask through. "It'll numb you and you might even be able to sleep a little. You're gonna feel rough tomorrow, though."

He took the flask and twisted the top open, holding it under his nose as he took a small whiff. Then he held it to his lips and upturned it to swallow every last drop.

"Well, that's one way to do it," I muttered. "You'll start feeling it soon."

The kid was so thin, he already began to sway where he sat. His lids half-closed and his brow finally relaxed.

"Hey, before you nod off," I said. "What's your name?"

His eyes snapped open, staring at me with their odd-colored gaze. For the first time, he looked confused. As if he didn't understand the question.

"I'm Alejandro de Leon," I offered. "But you can call me Jandro."

His expression relaxed again as he leaned heavily against the door.

"You can call me Shadow."

MARIPOSA

PRESENT DAY

I flopped over in bed, my hand slapping down on someone's hard, muscular body. As my eyes cracked open, my waking brain registered that this body was covered in short, dense fur.

Sure enough, Hades grinned at me with his goofy Doberman smile before licking my face. "Ugh, dog breath," I groaned, rolling away for fresh air and to finish joining the waking world.

The palm trees cast long shadows over the desert landscape, which meant I slept for several hours. Reaper left to interrogate the outpost guard before I went down for a nap and still hadn't come back.

I sat up, rubbing my face in an attempt to let the events of the last twenty-four hours sink in and solidify in my mind.

There was an explosion, and not a minute later, the

outpost guards descended on the Steel Demons MC, despite that we'd come peacefully as guests.

My heart skipped a beat at the notion that I included myself in that *we*, but was I part of them, really? I came as their medic, and I could still feel the ache of having Reaper between my legs earlier this morning.

My life flipped upside down in an instant, but several aspects remained the same. I still provided medical services, my latest patient being the massive Doberman in the bed next to me. I still traveled the Southwest, only I rode on the back of a roaring motorcycle instead of by foot or bus.

And just like before, I was surrounded by deadly men who killed with no hesitation. Only this time, I wasn't one of their targets. To make matters even more fun, I slept with the Steel Demons president. Making sense of my feelings for him or any of these men seemed as productive as unraveling a spider's web.

On the bright side, the Steel Demons were easy on the eyes and had no intention of killing me, since I was apparently useful.

I shook my head with a sigh and slid my feet down to the floor. These kinds of things shouldn't be thought about on an empty stomach and I was *starving*.

Hades lifted his head off the pillow, watching me as I got dressed.

"You stay here, boy," I told him. "I'll bring you something from the kitchen."

He was having none of that. As I headed for the door, he rolled over and jumped off the bed.

"No!"

I yelled too late, not that he would obey a command from me anyway. But I just put sixteen stitches in his flank to close up a shrapnel wound from the explosion.

"Hades, you can't go jumping," I scolded as he approached. "Your wound needs to heal."

I went to look at it and my heart nearly stopped.

"What the fuck?" I ran my hand over the shaved section of fur just above the incision. "How did you heal so fast?"

He wasn't fully healed, but the progress looked much further than just a few hours. Both sides of the incision had already sealed together, and shiny scar tissue was beginning to form.

I sat on the floor, stunned out of my damn mind. It should have been weeks before it looked like that. On top of his freakish ability to run alongside Reaper's bike without stopping, it became all too clear that nothing was ordinary about this dog.

"How long have I been asleep?" I asked his toothy grin. "Really now. Did I get put under some sleeping beauty spell and only your kiss could wake me up?"

He leaned forward and licked my face, assaulting me with slobber and dog breath again.

"Ugh, I knew it," I laughed, rolling backwards. "Your breath smells like the underworld itself, but you're the only prince around here."

He pranced around me playfully, eyes bright and alert. The drugs I gave him had worn off and he seemed like a brand-new pup.

"Well, if you're feeling better," I climbed to my feet. "I guess you can come with me on my quest for food."

He let out an excited yip and immediately went to the door. We left Reaper's suite together, Hades' back nearly brushing my hip as we made our way down the quiet halls.

I was honestly relieved to have him with me. The Steel Demons escaped the outpost guards and rescued me, Reaper, and a badly injured Hades from a ravine just outside the property. Reaper told me it was safe to walk around now, which I took as code to mean they killed everyone in retaliation for their capture.

Everyone except for that guard now being interrogated in their custody, and who knew what his fate would be in the hands of these men?

Despite the threat of danger gone, the eerie quietness of the place set me on high alert. My sandaled feet and Hades' claws were the only sounds echoing off the sandstone tiles and columns. The kitchen was just as quiet as I pushed open the swinging door.

I went immediately to the large refrigerator while Hades sniffed along the supply shelf on the opposite wall.

He's probably starving, too, I realized as I scanned the produce and prepped ingredients in sealed containers. Meat and dairy was scarce, but if I could find some rice or potatoes, he would probably make do with that for a little while.

I pulled open a drawer and almost shouted with excitement. Eggs! A good source of protein and calories for dogs and humans. Running my hands over the various shades of brown shells, I counted more than thirty in the carton. It had to be insanely difficult to get fresh eggs from a farmer this far up in the mountains. The more plausible answer was this place had its own chicken coop.

"Hades!" I whistled as I grabbed two eggs in each hand. "Want a yummy scramble for—"

A threatening growl and a whimper cut me off. I set the eggs down on the counter and darted in the direction of the sound. "Hades, what—"

Tucked back in a corner of the kitchen, a girl sat on the floor with her knees to her chest. Hades' teeth were bared as he snarled inches away from her face.

"Hades, back off!"

He ignored me, naturally, so I pushed him out of the way and kneeled between him and the girl.

"Hey, he won't hurt you. He's just protective. Are you okay?"

She lifted her head just a few inches and nodded, peering at me over her knees. I recognized her as one of the kitchen girls who served us when we first arrived.

"No one's going to hurt you." I placed a hand on her arm in an attempt to soothe her. "My name's Mariposa."

"They killed everyone," she said in a shaky whisper.

"It's...it's not what it seems." I sounded like I was making really lame excuses for the MC's carnage, and maybe I was. "The club was deceived by the owner of this place. They retaliated and won. But you weren't involved. They don't hurt innocents, I promise you."

Her head lifted another few inches. "They won't... take me?"

How was I supposed to answer that? They took me,

albeit not in the way she was probably thinking. I was afraid of that too at first, but by the time Reaper slid inside me, I wanted him just as badly as he did me.

While my feelings were a jumbled mess, I knew I could trust the Steel Demons president and his men to not hurt this girl. So I clasped my hand over hers and chose to reassure her.

"They won't touch you. I swear it."

"You better not fucking touch her!"

I turned my head slightly to see a gun barrel hovering in my peripheral vision.

"Step away!" the gun wielder demanded. "Back up slowly."

I did as instructed, finding out the gun's owner was the second kitchen worker as I backed up to the counter.

"Take it easy," I breathed, hands raised and eyes locked on the long, dark barrel pointed at my chest. "No one's hurting anyone."

Hades did not get the memo to calm down. He turned fearlessly to the girl with the gun, teeth bared and a low growl in his chest. It was enough for her eyes to cast a nervous flicker toward him, but she kept her focus on me.

"You're with them," she spat at me. "The road pirates who came here and killed everyone."

"Rightfully so because *your* boss was going to kill them first," I shot back. "Don't act like your side is so innocent in this."

"All we do is cook! We don't have much of a choice in what side we pick."

"Then put the gun down," I told her. "Because we're

not your enemies. Shoot that thing at me or the bikers and you'll make enemies, though."

Her wide eyes darted with indecision as the barrel lowered just slightly. I couldn't blame the girl for feeling conflicted. Like me, she probably made it this far by not trusting anyone.

When she didn't lower it fast enough, Hades made an attempt to speed up the process.

By biting her hand.

"Ahh! Get it off!" she screamed as the gun clattered to the floor.

I held my breath as I watched the weapon fall and then kicked it away. Hades immediately released her hand and sat on his haunches like a good boy. He returned my bewildered stare with innocent, large eyes. The damn dog really was just making sure she'd drop the gun.

"I'm fucking bleeding!" the girl wailed, curling her hand to her chest. "Get the bandages!" she yelled to her friend, quiet as a statue still sitting on the floor.

"Let me see," I reached out for her arm and gave her an annoyed look when she pulled away. "You're lucky I'm a trained medic. If you want to handle a dog bite on your own, be my guest."

She stared me down with her best defiant look before relenting, holding her injured hand out to me.

"Let's wash it in the sink," I suggested, walking around the island counter. "If you have a first aid kit, you can grab that," I told the other girl.

"This doesn't mean we're going to service any of

those men you came with," the injured woman hissed through gritted teeth as I washed the blood off.

"You're not expected to. Just do the same kitchen work you've been doing while we stay." I looked up and met her eyes. "Like I told your friend, they won't touch you."

Her eyes narrowed at me. "You shouldn't stay long, anyway. Our food stores are low."

"Really, now? When you're this far into the mountains?" I countered, scrubbing her puncture wounds with the soap bar. "You had an awful lot of eggs from what I saw."

She squirmed a little. "We have good relationships with farmers in the area. They make regular deliveries to us."

"In exchange for what?"

"Why are you so fucking nosy?" She pulled her hand from my grip. "I'm just saying your gang should leave if they don't want to starve. They're too big and have too many mouths to feed."

"It just doesn't make sense," I said coolly as I shut the water off. "A place this isolated would be a lot more likely to have its own food sources. You can't get *that* many fresh eggs without a chicken coop nearby."

"We don't have a chicken coop!" she insisted. "Those are to last us until the next delivery in a week. We just don't have enough for you, your dog, and all your men."

"And I think you're lying," I crossed my arms. "So how many chickens *do* you have? Any other livestock?"

"We don't have *any*—"

A clatter of metal on metal announced that her

friend just returned with a first aid kit and dropped it on the counter. But it was the soft flapping sound that followed that drew mine and Hades' attention to the open window.

"Ahhh!" both girls screamed as Gunner's falcon, Horus, flew into the kitchen and skidded across the counter with his limp victim in his talons.

"What is that?" the first girl whimpered as Horus began plucking at his bloodied carcass on the kitchen counter like this was his roost all along.

Hades let out an excited bark, propping his front paws on the counter to sniff out his feathered friend's conquest. Horus had already made serious headway on tearing his prey open, but the downy feathers in the air, scaly feet, and short beak gave it away.

The falcon caught a chicken for dinner. And Hades gave him puppy eyes like he was asking him to share.

I turned slowly to the kitchen girl whose face paled as she watched the scene before us.

Maybe it was rude of me but I was completely unable to help the smugness in my voice.

"You were saying?"

MARIPOSA

The kitchen girls, whose names I found out to be Marnie and Mimi, gave me no trouble after that. They showed me their small farm hidden at the bottom of a hill on the far side of the outpost —far away from all the guest rooms and accommodations.

In addition to about thirty adult chickens, they also had a small herd of goats, vegetable patches and fruit trees. Some supplies still required trading with other farmers but as I suspected, this place was largely self-sufficient.

When I asked Mimi, the girl who'd been bitten, if they could make chicken for the Steel Demons that evening, she was a lot more accommodating than before.

Horus gorged himself on his kill but left most of it on the counter, seeing as he wasn't a huge bird himself. The girls were thoroughly grossed out by the mess he made and refused to touch it. So I took to cooking up the leftovers with a mix of egg, rice, and a few vegetables for Hades.

"Why are you so cute?" I laughed as his stubby tail and whole rear end wiggled excitedly. "How do you know this is for you, huh?"

I put the food mixture in a clean, metal bowl and set it on the floor next to him, along with a bowl of water. As he scarfed down everything like he hadn't eaten in weeks, the healing scar on his flank caught my attention again. With him distracted by food, I ran a hand down his side as if touching him would reveal the trick my eyes were playing on me. But nothing changed. At this rate, he would be fully healed within two days.

Right then someone pushed forcefully through the kitchen door, making it bounce off the wall. The kitchen girls screamed.

"Thought I'd find you two together," Reaper's deep, gravelly voice traveled through the air and reached my ears like a caress. "Didn't think it'd be in here, though."

"I got hungry," I replied with a shrug, despite my pulse elevating with each step he took closer to me. "Hades decided to come with."

Reaper's bright green eyes dropped from my face to his dog, now licking his food bowl clean.

"He's walking already?" The Steel Demons president ran a hand down the dog's back, patting his ribs.

"More than that. Look," I pointed to the incision, "it's already closed up and scarring over. A week's worth of healing in hours."

Reaper looked pleased, but otherwise completely unsurprised. "You always were a fast healer, huh, boy?"

It was more than fast healing. I was pretty certain it was physically impossible. Just like running alongside a motorcycle going eighty miles per hour, for *hours*.

But before I could bring up any of this, Reaper pinned me with a stare that caught my breath in my throat.

"You weren't waiting for me in bed, like I told you to." He patted Hades out of the way to stand right in front of me with my back pinned to the kitchen counter.

"I told you, I got hungry."

"Mm." He rested his fingers gently on the edge of my jaw while his thumb stroked across my lower lip. "So did I."

"Lucky for you," I tilted my head just out of contact with his hand, "they have chickens here. We'll be eating well during our stay."

"That's not what I'm hungry for." A slow, devious smile formed on his lips. "You two," he addressed the kitchen girls for the first time. "Leave. Give us ten, no, five minutes."

Mimi's eyes darted back and forth just as they did when I told her to put the gun away. This time, she did as was asked much faster, scurrying out through the back doors with Marnie on her heels.

"What are you doi—"

My question was cut off by Reaper's mouth smothering mine just as he lifted me by the waist to sit on the counter. Flying to his shoulders for balance, my hands gripped the smooth, well-worn leather of his cut. His kiss was harsh, roughened by the dark stubble growing on his face. And still I held on and pulled him closer to deepen it.

"Hades, go." His mouth broke away to give the command and returned to conquer mine before I had a chance to take a breath.

"You want to do this *here*?" I panted when his lips dragged across my cheek to my earlobe, his fingers already hooking in the waistband of my pants.

"Sugar, I want you anywhere and everywhere," he chuckled with a nip to my ear. "But I'm about to hold church and only have a few minutes."

His mouth returned to mine as he stripped my lower half bare. The stainless steel counter was cold against my heated flesh and my mind still reeled with the question of what exactly Reaper wanted. A quickie? He stepped away when I reached for his belt buckle, bending at the waist to place a soft kiss on my thigh with a devilish smile.

Oh.

That was what he meant when he said he was hungry.

He pulled my hips forward with a grunt, making me lean back on my elbows and bringing my pussy right up to his face. Which seemed to be just where he wanted it.

He kissed me there with just as much need and passion as he kissed my mouth. My head fell back wantonly with a moan and he answered with a, "hmmm," of his own against my tender flesh. The vibration of his voice on my skin ignited every nerve in my body. I found myself raising my hips, pressing myself harder against his mouth in a silent plea for more.

Reaper's lips pulled back into a smile as a throaty chuckle escaped him. His eyes, hooded with desire, lifted to meet mine.

"Enjoying yourself?" He slid a hand down my thigh to press achingly slow circles around my clit.

"I can think of worse ways to spend my time," I panted, matching his cocky grin. God forbid this man's ego get any bigger. We'd all be crushed under the weight of it if that happened.

"I see," he mused with mock thoughtfulness as his hand moved lower, stroking through my wet folds until he found my entrance.

His eyes remained locked on mine as he pressed a finger inside me, then another. It was the most intense game of don't-blink-first as his fingers curled up to stroke my channel. He held me captive with that green gaze as he toyed with me, alternating between hard and fast, slow and gentle.

I was biting into my lip so hard, I was seconds away from tasting blood. When my lids fluttered closed and my head fell back again, I knew I'd lost. His soft laugh against my skin was cocky with his victory.

He pressed another kiss to my thigh right before dragging his lips to the small bundle of nerves that had been begging for attention since he first walked in. The moment his mouth sealed over my clit, I knew I was done for. He rendered me powerless with just his mouth and hands and it felt wholly unfair.

Rolling my hips shamelessly against his face, I raked my nails through the dark hair of his scalp, wishing I could touch more of him. Maybe then I'd have a shot at having him at my mercy for a change.

Reaper was a fair man, but I never pegged him as especially generous. So why he was pleasing me so selflessly, I couldn't be sure. Would he want something in return later?

My tongue wet my lips at the thought of taking his long, hard length into my mouth. I could see the shape of it now, practically punching a hole in his jeans. All men loved blowjobs, but could I reduce the almighty Reaper to a quivering mess like he was doing to me right now? Would he ever allow such a thing?

His skilled suction of my clit and rhythmic stroking of his fingers in and out of me took me right to the edge, but it was the thought of him at the mercy of my mouth that pushed me over.

Stars danced in my vision as my body convulsed with release. He let out another pleased hum against my clit as my pussy closed around his fingers. He pulled his hand out of me with a wet sucking sound and licked both his fingers.

"Delicious," he purred, standing to his full height.

I stared up at him, spread-eagle and exposed on the counter as I fought to catch my breath.

"I take it you want the favor returned?" My eyes fell to the bulge in his pants, my mouth already watering for it.

"Later," he said, kneeling to help me back into my pants. "I'm already late for church."

"Oh, right. You said that." I swore my orgasms before this never made me sound so dumb. All the blood rushing to my clit must have deprived my brain of oxygen.

I hopped down from the counter and smoothed my hands down my clothes, like I was going to fool anyone that Reaper and I had just been telling knock-knock jokes.

He grabbed my shirt in his fist and pulled me in for another kiss, with his lips and tongue still coated in my arousal and just as possessive as ever.

"I just had to taste you," he murmured with a light flick of his tongue against my lips before he pulled away. "You seriously better be waiting in my bed tonight. Or there'll be no more coming for you, sugar."

He grinned at my resulting frown, then playfully tapped me on the nose before turning to leave the kitchen.

"Hades!" he called, followed by a high-pitched whistle. Not a second later, I heard the trotting of four feet alongside his master.

Reaper left me so hot and bothered, I realized I completely forgot to ask about the man they'd been interrogating.

And possibly torturing.

THREE

GUNNER

F ucking motherfucker of all fucking fucks. We were utterly and completely fucked, and not in the good way.

I barely took note of everyone filing into the conference room for church. My thoughts were too fucking loud. If what Fischlin's guard said was true, the entire wellbeing of the club was at risk.

No, not just the club. Sheol. Our home, the women and kids, everyone. And it all fell on my shoulders.

I trusted General Tash. Every deal we ever made had gone smoothly, no bumps or issues. He seemed like a fair guy, never asking for too much, nor trying to undercut us on our goods. The agreement we had seemed to be mutually beneficial. So why would he turn around and try to fuck us with a cactus? None of it made any sense.

A hand clapped down on my shoulder, jolting me out of my hamster wheel of thoughts.

"Not your fault, man," Jandro muttered as he sank

into the chair next to me. Shadow slipped into the one on the other side of him without making a sound. "We'll figure it out."

"I need a fucking drink, bro," I sighed, dropping my forehead into my hands. "This is such bullshit."

"It's gonna be all right," he patted my back. "Plenty of other generals are looking for black market supplies. We have plenty to choose from."

"Tash was supposed to be one of the trustworthy ones," I groaned. "How many did we vet before going with him? A fuck-ton."

"Where the fuck is Reaper?" Jandro swiveled his chair to look around the room, only to be met with shrugs.

"Probably getting his dick examined by the medic," Big G snorted from across the table.

"She has to find it first," Dallas added, earning him chuckles from everyone except me, Jandro, and Shadow.

Then again, I didn't know if Shadow could laugh even if he was given step-by-step instructions.

"Motherfucker," Jandro slapped his palms down on the table and rose to his feet just as Reaper came through the doorway with Hades at his side.

"Sorry I'm late. Swung by the kitchen for a bite to eat."

The smirk he wore as he took his seat at the head of the table was more than telling. An exchanged glance with Jandro told me he was thinking the exact same thing.

"Close the doors. Church is in session." Reaper struck the gavel on the wooden table once before setting it down to rub his forehead. "We've got a lot to unpack here, boys. Let's start at the beginning. Jandro?"

"We arrived roughly two-and-a-half days ago," the vice president recounted. "Gunner, Reaper and I went in with an offering of ceramic-tipped arrows in exchange for three days' stay and the hopes of a future business relationship."

"How did Fischlin receive us, in your opinion?"

"As expected," Jandro shrugged. "He seemed surprised by our visit, and not pleasantly so. But he came around after seeing what we offered and the deal went smoothly."

"Gunner?" Reaper turned to face me. "Would you agree with that assessment?"

"I would, President. It wasn't until we stayed a full day that I noticed Fischlin's guards keeping an especially close eye on us. And they were already utilizing the arrows we gave."

"I went up to the lounge to smoke after Jandro and I went for a ride that morning," Reaper continued. "One of the kitchen girls fetched me saying Fischlin wanted to discuss something right then. On my way over there, the explosion knocked Hades and me into the ravine."

"We heard it and sent Mariposa over the wall before they swarmed in on us," Jandro picked up where he left off. "At the pool we had no weapons, so we surrendered and allowed them to lock us up. We remained there until Shadow let us out."

"Shadow," Reaper addressed the large, silent man to Jandro's right. "Where were you while this was happening?"

The whole table fell silent. Shadow's jaw ticked as his dark eye slid over to Jandro, who gave him a nudge and an encouraging nod. The big guy didn't like to talk, especially at the church table, so we waited patiently for his piece.

"I was in my room when I heard the explosion," Shadow began. "I waited there while they captured the rest of you—"

"Yeah, thanks for the help," Big G interrupted to scoff at him. "Hiding out while they rounded up your brothers and took us prisoner."

"Hey," Jandro snapped. "Unless you've got something useful to say, keep your fuckin' mouth shut."

"Both of you shut the fuck up," Reaper pounded the table with his gavel before nodding at Shadow. "Go on."

"I had to catch them unaware to maximize the efficiency of an attack," Shadow stared directly at Big G. "Otherwise, I would have been captured like the rest of you and then *no one* would get you out."

"Big G's just being a big prick," Jandro glared across the table. "Everyone here knows how you operate. Keep going, man."

"A few hours after taking all of you, they began searching the rooms," Shadow continued. "They shouted loudly about finding the woman—"

"Mariposa," I muttered under my breath. For some reason it irked me how Shadow talked about her. I couldn't place my finger on it exactly, but he made her sound like an object. *The woman*, like she was some obstacle we had to deal with.

"Their shouting and carelessness made them easy

targets," Shadow went on. "I knifed the man who got into my room, took his bow and quiver, then killed everyone in my way until I reached you all."

"Did you really sneak up on every single one of them?" Dallas asked in wide-eyed fascination.

"A few saw me right before they died," Shadow shrugged.

"Once Shadow got us out, we took weapons out of the armory," I decided to pick up the storytelling next. "One of the guards ran up to us in surrender, saying Fischlin was escaping with someone. We ran toward his office, saw where the explosion happened, but we were too late to catch him."

"He was on the back of someone's bike riding south," Jandro added. "They were too far away to see a patch on the cut."

"And our surrendered guard tells us General Tash has been here multiple times," Reaper drummed his fingers on the tabletop. "Pumping tons of resources into this place. Giving them solar panels, high-quality building materials, even chickens and goats for food. All to fuck us over. Why?"

"Another question," Jandro piped up. "How did he know we were coming?"

"Gunner," Reaper's gaze snapped to me. "When was your last contact with the general?"

"Same as everyone's, when we made our deal in Navajo almost two weeks ago. Right before we stopped in Old Phoenix for the last time." *And brought ourselves home a pretty little medic.*

"You're sure?" The question came from Big G. My

head snapped over to him, the edges of my vision already tinged with red.

"Yeah, I'm fucking sure, G. You think I would keep secrets from the club? From *my brothers?*"

"I dunno, man. I'm just sayin'." The fucker leaned back in his seat as he backpedaled. "You're the one in charge of making the deals and shit. Maybe Tash wasn't too happy about something and—"

I was on my feet and my fists hit the table before I could stop myself.

"I'm your *captain*, you pussy son-of-a-bitch! You want to throw accusations at me? Get over here and back that shit up! Be a fucking man!"

The whole room broke out into a chorus of discernable yells, but I tuned it all out. I couldn't even hear myself. My only goal was to feel the satisfying crunch of my fist into Big G's skull. But someone grabbed me and held me back before I could reach the motherfucker.

"I said, ENOUGH!" Reaper bellowed with a raised hand.

Everyone quieted down, our ragged breaths the only sounds in the room as everyone looked to the president.

"Church is adjourned until everyone can fucking get ahold of themselves," Reaper snarled, his eyes scanning over all of us. "That goes for all of you. No digs at what anyone did or didn't do. No accusations without solid proof. Get the fuck out of my sight."

"Gun, you gonna be cool?" Jandro asked, indicating he was the one holding me back.

"Yeah," I didn't take my eyes off of Big G. "I'm good."

He released me and I straightened my clothes right before pointing at the loudmouthed piece of shit. "You're out of my guard. I'm giving your post to someone *loyal* when we get back."

"Gunner," Reaper cut in, stepping in front of him before he could respond. "A word?"

I blew out a long breath, pushing my hair back as I nodded. "Yeah. 'Course, president."

He clapped me on the back, leading me out of the room and toward an open balcony overlooking the pool. Reaching into his cut, he pulled out his cigarette case and offered me one. I accepted it and took a big drag the moment he lit the end for me.

"Anything you want to tell me, Gun?" The slim, black cigarette bobbed between Reaper's lips as he spoke.

I exhaled a plume of white smoke, leaning against one of the columns as the nicotine hit my brain.

"Nothing that'll help," I said before taking another drag. "I'm just worried, Reap. Our whole community depends on me for goods. Now I have to scramble to take care of our people." I hissed a breath through my teeth as a fresh surge of anger hit me. "I know what it looks like since I've had the most contact with Tash out of all of us, but fuck, man."

Reaper watched me silently, pale smoke swirling around him.

"You know I'm loyal, Reap," I said. "I've bled for this club. I'm a Steel Demon to my core. I would never, ever fuck us over."

"I believe you, Gun." Reaper turned and leaned his

forearms over the balcony. "But someone within us *has* fucked us over." He glanced down at Hades guarding us faithfully before asking in a low voice, "Have you seen anything suspicious through Horus?"

"Nothing out of the ordinary since we got here," I answered with the same low tone. "I'll keep looking, though."

"Make sure you watch *everyone*," Reaper ordered under his breath. "Even Jandro, Mariposa. Hell, even me."

"Narcing on yourself, President?" I asked with a dry laugh.

"It's like how those old mysteries used to go," he chuckled as he tossed his cigarette butt over the balcony. "Everyone's a suspect. Especially the one who seems the most innocent."

FOUR

MARIPOSA

With the guys wrapped up in their business and now Hades abandoning me to be with his master, I ran out of things to do.

My belly was full of food and my latest patient had been treated for her dog bite. I could keep wandering the empty halls of this place, hide out in my room, or relax by the pool.

Or you could strip down and wait in Reaper's bed for him, like he wanted you to.

I huffed to myself as I dug out a clean swimsuit and stripped out of my normal clothes. Not that the idea wasn't tempting, especially after what he did in the kitchen. But I still didn't want to make myself *that* available to him.

A man like him got bored if women offered themselves too easily. His confrontation with Heather showed me that. He'd just jump to the next girl if I came to his every beck and call. I already figured he'd discard me for something new and shiny eventually. He all but promised me that with the whole, "I don't do traditional relationships" pitch.

But I had to admit I was enjoying my tryst with the Steel Demons president and wanted to make it last. And if I remained a career medic with the club, I had to accept the doggish behavior of its members. At least they didn't coerce women into bed with them and generally seemed trustworthy.

After getting into my suit, my pulse sped up as I walked out onto the pool deck. This was where everything happened. The explosion. Guards swarming in. Gunner looking like he was having a seizure.

I dragged a deck chair over to the sun and sank into it, keeping the doors in my peripheral vision. I had nothing to fear now but still felt the need to check my exits.

The hot, dry desert air parched my throat. I closed my eyes and imagined a margarita. Texas had several dry counties even before the Collapse, but the teetotalers wasted no time in coming out of the woodwork afterward. Nearly half of the former state of Texas forbade alcohol by the time I graduated school, which only created a black market for it. Beer was easy enough to make and no one cared much about how it tasted, but distilling liquor was more difficult. Especially on a large scale. Authentic tequila from Mexico cost a small fortune.

My dad had a bottle stashed away that we hoarded like gold. The last time I tasted tequila was when we took shots on my twenty-first birthday.

"There's three rules—lick, swallow, suck, but no one tells you the fourth one," Dad warned me.

"What's that?" I asked.

"Don't tell your mom," he laughed, pinching my cheek. "She'll kill me."

A splash pulled me out of my memories, prompting me to crack one eye open. I was greeted by the sight of Gunner cutting elegantly through the pool. He did several laps back and forth of a sleek butterfly stroke. It looked absolutely beautiful, but exhausting as hell.

His long arm swept through the water, every muscle flexed. He wore the Steel Demons horned skull tattoo on his upper back, the edges of the design stretching out to the backs of his arms. With the way he moved, it almost looked like demonic black wings spread across his back.

A demonic angel. How fitting.

Powerful kicks of his legs drove him up before crashing down. I lost count of how many laps he did, but he didn't stop until he looked ready to slip beneath the surface.

He held onto the edge of the pool with one hand, chest expanding with hard, ragged breaths. I startled when he punched the pool wall with his other hand, muttering curses to himself.

It wasn't until then that I realized the sunniest, most cheerful of the demons was seriously pissed off.

I lowered my feet to the ground and stood, walking tentatively toward the pool's edge. He flashed a smile as soon as he saw me, but I saw the grimace underneath.

"Hey, Mari," he greeted, shielding his eyes from the

sun. "You are a sight to behold," he added, taking in my bikini.

I ignored his comment and sat on the edge, dipping my feet into the water next to him.

"Let me see your hand."

"Sweet of you to worry," he chuckled. "But it's nothing, baby girl. Church was just frustrating, that's all."

"I'm not leaving you alone until you let me see."

"Well, that's fine with me," he grinned, dipping his head back so his blond hair spread across the surface. "I like you right where you are."

"Come on, Gunner," I extended my hand to him. "I saw blood in the water. Give it."

"Hmm," he pretended to consider it for a moment. "Only because I'll never turn down a pretty girl holding my hand."

I couldn't think of a snappy comeback, so I distracted myself with examining his scraped knuckles while the flush creeped up my neck and into my cheeks.

"You'll be fine. Just don't make a habit out of punching solid walls."

I released his hand, but he kept it in my lap for a few seconds before letting it drop back into the pool. Water droplets trailed from my knees down my calves like fingertips.

"I won't." His voice carried an edge of seriousness. "I just had to pretend it was someone's face."

"Whose?"

"Doesn't matter. Hey!" His grin returned as he tickled along the bottoms of my feet. "Want your first swim lesson?"

"No!" I kicked toward his chest, hitting him with a good splash. "Not after that stunt you pulled."

This guy picked me up and dropped me in the pool *before* I had a chance to say I couldn't swim.

"I won't do that again, promise." He went serious again, grabbing my foot and giving it a gentle squeeze. "I'll just show you how to float on your back. Super simple."

I stopped kicking, enjoying his grip on my ankle more than I'd like to admit.

"You won't let me drown?"

"Cross my heart." He did the motion over his chest. "You trust me, Mari?"

I steeled myself, grabbing the edge just outside my knees. "Yeah, I do."

His smile lit up his eyes at that point, shining like two sapphires. "Okay. Hop in when you're ready."

We were at the shallow end, so I knew I'd hit the bottom safely. Still, I appreciated that he moved in front of me so I could hold onto his shoulders as I slid off the edge and into the water.

"I got you." Gunner placed a gentle hold on my waist until my feet hit the bottom.

"Okay," I breathed, looking up at him. "Now what?" The closeness of him was overwhelming, and yet the safest place to be.

"Turn this way." He guided me with a hand on the back of my arm until the side of my body faced his chest. "Now start leaning back like you're lying down in a bathtub."

"Uh..."

"Your feet are going to want to float up. Just let them. I've got your back." The weight of his hand pressed to my lower back. "I won't let you sink, Mari."

I nodded before grabbing his forearm with one hand and the pool ledge with the other. "Don't ask me to let go, 'cause I won't."

"That's all right," he smiled. "Hold onto me all you want."

I took a deep breath and started tilting my head back, the desert sky and tops of the palm trees entering my vision.

"Keep breathing. Just relax," Gunner instructed. "Your ears will go underwater but not your face. You'll be able to breath the whole time."

I nodded and allowed the back of my head to kiss the surface of the water. My toes stretched out along the bottom, curling to hold onto the sensation of solid ground. Gunner's hands on my back helped, but I was still scared to let go.

"Look straight up. Let your feet come up," he repeated gently. "I've got you."

When I leaned my head back just another inch, that was when my ears went below the surface and my feet lifted off the ground. I squeezed Gunner's forearm in a moment of panic. I couldn't hear him anymore!

But he leaned over me, looking down with a smile and mouthed, "Good job."

His voice was warbled and distorted but I could hear him after all, which was a huge relief.

"Am I doing it?" I asked, probably too loudly. "Am I floating?"

"You're doing it, baby girl."

He took one hand away from my back, which scared me into death-gripping his arm again, only until he pressed upward softly on my calves to float my legs higher.

"You're doing it on your own," he beamed down at me. "You don't need to hold onto anything."

"Don't let me go!"

"I won't." He leaned closer to me, the tips of his wet hair brushing my skin. "Promise I won't."

Goddamn, his eyes were gorgeous. And his smile. And...everything. He was such a beautiful specimen of a human being. I didn't notice how shamelessly I stared at him until he pulled back, looking at something in the distance.

"Ready to come up?"

I nodded and he returned both hands to my back, tilting me upward slowly until my feet found solid ground once again.

"That wasn't so bad, was it?" he grinned, lowering into the water until only his shoulders were exposed.

"I had a good set of training wheels," I laughed, wringing out my hair.

"You can totally do it on your own," he assured me. "I think your fear is worse than what you're actually afraid of. Like, what's that saying?" He ran his hands through his hair, creating drops and rivulets running down his neck. "The only thing to fear is fear itself. I think one of the early presidents said that."

"Can't decide if those are words of wisdom or total bullshit," I teased, aiming a splash at him.

He lifted a shoulder in a shrug. "There's a fine line between both, maybe."

A few moments of silence passed between us, with water lapping at the pool's edges as the only sound.

"Hey," I voiced softly. "Thanks, Gunner. I've never been able to do that before."

"Sure thing, baby girl." He looked toward the direction of the kitchen. "Think I'll head in for some grub. I heard chicken's on the menu. You coming?"

"I already ate, but thanks," I answered. "I got to watch Horus tear apart a whole chicken earlier."

"He's a savage," Gunner laughed. "That beak does not lend to careful eating. Sorry if that grossed you out."

"I have zero issue with blood and guts everywhere. But I think the kitchen staff were mildly traumatized."

"Ah. It's on them to get used to it then," he grinned, lifting himself out of the pool with one strong push of his long arms. "Have a good night, Mari. Keep practicing your float."

"You, too. Thanks again, Gun."

As he toweled himself off, he cast a downward smile that almost seemed shy. "I should thank you, too."

"For what?"

His eyes flickered up to meet mine. "For trusting me."

FIVE

REAPER

Never before had I ever seen my club so divided.

I was so careful to make the Steel Demons an army of *men*. A brotherhood that could trust each other, who could work seamlessly as a single unit. Now, someone I vetted and trusted was a backstabbing piece of shit. Someone in this dining room *knew* General Tash wanted to fuck us, and told that slimy shit bag we were coming.

And I had no idea who.

At dinner, people broke off to eat in pairs or by themselves, eyeballing everyone else with suspicion. No one received more stink-eyes than Gunner.

On the surface, he appeared to take it all in stride. He met the stares with defiance and never gave off a hint of guilt. But I knew it ate him up inside that his brotherhood, his chosen family, suspected him of betrayal so quickly.

He took up one of the low couches with his chicken burrito, pitcher of beer, and loyal falcon at his shoulder.

His feet stretched out on the coffee table, crossed leisurely at the ankles. He was making it clear he belonged here and it was one of these other sneaky fuckers that didn't.

Only Shadow sat near him, devouring chicken tacos in between swigs of vodka. They didn't speak, but I knew without a doubt Shadow's presence close by was a silent move of solidarity. Those two weren't the closest in the club but the mutual respect between them was strong.

A plate clattered near my beer, followed by Jandro sliding into the seat next to me.

"You trust Gunner?" he asked before taking a large bite of his chicken taco.

"Yes," I answered without hesitation. "You trust Shadow?"

"Yes." He washed his food down with my untouched beer. "So it's safe to assume the weasel isn't one of us four?"

"I'm certain it isn't." I'd known Jandro nearly my whole life, and Gunner only a few years less. I knew Shadow the least of anyone, but if Jandro trusted him, that was all I needed.

"I asked Gun to have Horus keep a close eye on everyone," I said. "Including me."

"You?" Jandro scoffed. "Why?"

"I guaran-fuckin'-tee you someone thinks *I'm* the cause of this. If we're gonna have a witch hunt, no one can be exempt."

"Does that include Mariposa?"

I leaned back against a column, taking note of her

absence in the dining room. Why wasn't she here? More specifically, why wasn't she lying back on this table, serving me up that sweet pussy for dessert?

"No one suspects it's her," I answered. "She has no power in the club and hasn't been with us long enough to know about our dealings."

"Is that what *you* think?" Jandro's gaze on me was heavy. "Has she really embraced being with us or is she still trying to find a way to escape us?"

I didn't have an immediate answer for him and he noticed.

"She's been with us a couple of weeks now," I sighed, rubbing my eyes. "And in that time, I haven't asked her what *she* wants."

Jandro tilted his head at me. "Whether or not it has anything to do with this, that might be worth finding out."

I FOUND Mariposa in my suite, which delighted me immensely. But rather than naked in my bed, she was dressed in a pair of shorts and a tank top, sitting in an armchair in the entry room.

Hades went to her immediately, forcing her to put her book down as he practically jumped into her lap.

"Hey, good boy! How are you?" she cooed, rubbing the sides of his face before placing a kiss on his snout.

"You're going to spoil him rotten," I groaned, kicking my boots off in the doorway.

"Good. He deserves it." She continued scratching

him, making sure to get his ears and his belly as he twisted, contorted, and squeezed to get his big body snuggled up next to her.

He laid his head on her stomach and looked at me, smiling blissfully as if to say, *Oh yes. I deserve this.*

"And what does his master get, hmm?" I shrugged off my cut and draped it over the back of a chair.

"I don't know," Mari watched me with caution as I approached her. "His master doesn't strike me as a good boy."

"He better fucking not," I growled, curling my fist in the hair at her nape as I leaned over to steal a kiss from her.

She played a tough chick, acting like she could push my buttons and pretend like she didn't want me *that* badly. But I tasted it in the way her mouth melted against mine. Her skin flushed with heat. She may not have been in bed, but she'd been sitting here a while watching that door for me to come through.

I nudged Hades off of the chair so I could scoop her up. She smiled against my mouth as I lifted her in my arms, carrying her to the bedroom.

"How was church?" Her lips moved to my neck.

"Can't tell you that." I set her down on the bed and gave a swat to her ass. "Church is sacred. Top secret information privy only to those who attend."

She gave me a look over her shoulder. "Gunner seemed upset."

"Yeah," I sighed, pulling apart my belt. "Shit is just kind of tense right now, in light of recent events."

"The owner trying to kill you guys."

"Yeah, that." I slid a palm over her waist. "And trying to capture you. To sell or use you, no doubt."

She rolled over to face me, propping her elbow up. We were both lying on our sides with our legs dangling over the edge of the bed. At some point the mood shifted from expecting hot, sweaty sex to cuddling and pillow talk.

And I honestly didn't mind it.

"What did you do to the guard?" she asked.

"Nothing." I grabbed her thigh to pull her closer and she ended up swinging her leg over my hip. "He spilled everything like a waterfall. We were able to verify he was being honest, too. No creative extraction necessary."

"So I don't need to examine him?" She raised a quizzical eyebrow.

"Nah," I chuckled. "You can have the night off, Miss Medic."

"What *are* you going to do with him?" Her hand slid over mine resting on the side of her leg.

"Dunno yet," I admitted. "Probably drop him off somewhere far away when we're done here. He's no good to Fischlin's people now. They'll kill him if they find him."

Her fingers skimmed up my arm, drifting over my shoulder and then my chest. I secretly loved that she enjoyed touching me so much. Too many women were afraid to express their own desires nowadays.

"What if you kept him?" Her eyes lifted to mine as she posed the question. "Brought him into the club?"

"Fuck no," I scoffed. "He is *not* Steel Demon material."

"Why not? He's honest, right? I know how much you value that."

I sucked in a breath. She had no idea how ironic that statement was, considering my current dilemma at hand.

"If he rolled over and talked to us so quickly, there's no stopping him from ratting us out to someone else," I explained. "My guys would never crack under interrogation. I know that for a fact."

"What if this was an out he'd been looking for?" she pressed. "Slavery isn't just for women and free labor. A lot of guys have been forced to become soldiers."

"Don't play that card with me, sugar," I sighed. "I got what I needed from him. I'm in no position to adopt another stray, as Noelle puts it."

"You already know he's a capable scout and archer." Mari's eyebrows lifted. "Do you have someone with those sets of talents in your club?"

"I have Gunner, who can hit a sparrow with a sling-shot from a hundred yards away." I chewed the inside of my cheek. What she didn't know was how busy Gun would be setting up new trade deals now that we no longer had Tash. The truth was, I *could* use another marksman.

"It still doesn't hurt to have a variety of talents, right?"

"God damn you, woman." I rolled onto my back, rubbing the heels of my palms into my eyes. "Why am I actually fucking considering this?"

"Because you know it's a good idea." She remained propped up on her elbow, her eyes traveling along the length of my torso stretched out on the bed. "You brought me on after all."

"I brought you on for your medical expertise, not for recruiting new members into my club." I rolled toward her, not stopping until I had her pinned beneath me. "But you have been beneficial in other ways."

She wriggled and shot me defiant looks but it was no true struggle. She was right where she wanted to be. The thought reminded me of what Jandro said in the dining room, and I halted the kiss I was about to plant on her.

"What do you want?"

She blinked up at me. "That's...an abrupt question."

"Do you actually *want* to be here? Or would you still run away at the first chance you got?"

Her gaze up at me was curious, trying to figure me out.

"Since when does what *I* want matter?" she asked. "You've never bothered to ask me this since tying me to you on your bike."

"I know. But I'm no slave owner, you told me that yourself. I truly don't want to keep you against your will, not if you'll take dangerous risks to escape." I was rambling now—my heart, mind, and mouth at war with how much I should say. "What you want *does* matter. To me, it does." I lowered my forehead to hers, our lips hovering less than an inch apart. "So tell me."

Her hands came up, wrapping around my shoulders.

"I want to heal those who've been hurt," she said, barely above a whisper. "I want to save lives and put fears to rest. I want to provide hope and a glimpse of humanity to those who see nothing but pain and loss."

Her nails scratched across my scalp. "As long as I get to do that, I guess it doesn't really matter where I am, does it?"

My body hovered tense above her. She answered my question in every way but how I wanted to hear it—did she want to be *here*, as part of my club, with *me?*

"We'll provide no shortage of patients for you to treat," I said in a clipped tone. "I can promise you that."

"Oh, don't get all grumpy on me." She lifted her lips to press a long, languid kiss to my mouth. "I'm not afraid you'll kill or torture me anymore, so no, I won't run away. And I've resigned to enjoying the perks of being with the Steel Demons." She shifted her legs underneath me until they straddled my waist, and my cock pressed against her core.

"*All* of the perks," she added in a sultry whisper.

SIX

MARIPOSA

I woke up with a heavy arm draped over my waist and a rhythmic, resting heartbeat against my naked back.

Reaper's breathing tickled the back of my neck. His other arm stretched out under my head, his bicep as my pillow. I didn't have to turn and look at him to know his hard, scowling expression was replaced with one of relaxation.

Careful not to disturb him, I pointed my toes and arched my back, letting out a soft groan in my stretch. The ache of last night's activities returned as my body roused, bringing a tiny smile to my face.

I'd never expect a man like Reaper to keep me but I chose to enjoy being his main course while it lasted. And now in the morning after, *enjoy* felt like quite the understatement.

He gave just as much as he took, which I should have realized after that surprise in the kitchen. Last night I lost track of the orgasms he gave me before chasing his own, and even after that, he held me against his rapid heartbeat, panting in my ear as his fingers found their way to my clit again.

A stallion in the sack, I expected. A healthy dose of tenderness with a near-obsession of getting me off? Quite unexpected.

I started rolling away, peeling my back from the heat of his chest only to feel his arm clamp down tighter around me.

"Where you goin'?" he murmured, voice gravelly with sleep.

"Clearly nowhere," I sighed under the weight of his arm. Come to think of it, he was being just as clingy as Hades.

"That's right." He brought the other arm to wrap in front of my shoulders, pulling my whole body back against his. "You're mine," he added with a smoldering kiss to my shoulder blade.

"Reaper..." Any protest I had came out shaky and weak, not due to the soreness in my body or lack of sleep. But because I *still* craved that stiff cock pressing against my ass, his mouth on my skin, and the way he moved against me.

"Reaper, I'm exhausted," I huffed, despite arching against him. "You barely let me sleep at all."

"I didn't hear you complaining last night," he teased, helping himself to a palmful of my ass.

"I think you broke me." I looked over my shoulder at him, unable to help the coy smile on my face.

"Then I have to fix you, don't I?" Green eyes, hooded with lust and sleep, met mine with a lazy grin.

"I'm no medical professional, but I know what you need."

"I *need* a cup of coffee and a shower."

"Mm, you'll get that, too." He slid a hand down the back of my thigh as he spooned me from behind. The next thing I felt was something hot and solid pressing against my sex.

"Reaper, I'm still sore." The words came out with a moan, but not as a complaint. I still wanted him, he just needed to know what he was working with.

"So stay like this." He held my legs closed as we laid flush together on our sides. "Just lie with me."

Did I detect a hint of sweetness there? Maybe a tiny shred of vulnerability? Whatever it was disappeared the moment I looked over my shoulder, and he captured my mouth in a savage kiss.

He kissed with no less confidence and possessiveness than always, but they weren't nearly as bruising. Not even when his lips moved to my nape, merely teasing my skin with light suction even though he knew how much I liked his roughness. His hands came to my breasts, kneading them with far more gentleness than the manhandling of last night.

I reached him where I could, bringing one arm back to wrap around his neck, but I could do little else in this position besides press back and move with him. He let out a groan between my shoulder blades, only thrusting enough to rub his cock along my sex without penetrating me. My flesh slicked with wetness and my core hollowed out. Even after a satisfying, vigorous night, I needed every inch of him.

"Reaper..." His name was a plea now, not a protest. If I had to be honest, it was never a protest.

"Mariposa," he answered, burying his face in my neck as his arms wrapped around my chest.

Every slick of him *not* entering me was pure torture. My pulse thrummed in anticipation for that delicious fill of him that never came.

"Reaperrr..."

"I love how you say my name," he growled. "I could tease you all day just to hear you beg."

"You wouldn't."

"Watch me."

Every time I tried opening my legs to give him access to slide in, he held them closed.

"You're depriving yourself, too, you know," I huffed in frustration.

"Nah, sugar," he nuzzled my cheek. "I'm just making the ending that much sweeter."

I leaned my head back on his shoulder, giving in to his control and relishing in all the sensations running through my body. His hands moved where he pleased, exploring me as if this was our first time together.

He kept us that way for as long as he could stand it. When he finally slipped inside me he shuddered against my back, fingers digging into my waist.

"Keep your legs closed," he moaned. "You're so tight like this, my God..."

The angle of our bodies forced him to take shallow thrusts, which I was grateful for. I couldn't handle another session of deep pounding, but this right now was...*nice.*

I loved the full length of his body pressed against me, the way he grabbed me and how he kissed all of my sensitive spots. It was all the best things that lazy morning sex should be.

And my clit, still sensitive and overworked from the night before, tingled with the onset of yet another orgasm just from the pressure of my thighs glued together.

"Fuck, why are you getting even tighter?" he growled with a soft chuckle to my ear. "My poor cock can't take how good you feel."

"I'm gonna come soon," I panted, my fists curling in the sheets.

"Still got a little left in you, huh?" He nipped my shoulder. "Let me feel it, sugar."

His hand began a slow, sensual descent down my belly before I smacked it away.

"I'm almost there, just don't stop."

"Mm, I love when you tell me that." His hand returned to my breast, rolling my aching nipple between his fingers as he kept on with his steady thrusts. The stamina and control he had was mind-boggling to me. He never came until I did at least once.

The gentle build-up between my thighs ramped up as Reaper teased my nipples. I began quivering, tingling in all of my extremities as he sucked my earlobe and moaned against my neck.

"Fuck, that's so beautiful," he rasped. "Come for me."

I pressed back on his thrusts with soft whimpers, desperate and frenzied for a release that was inching along far too slowly. Reaper never tried to rush me there. He wrapped around me like he could spend the rest of the day just touching and teasing me.

"Fuck," I panted, squeezing my trembling thighs together like a vice. I was chasing a feeling that was always just out of reach.

"Relax, sugar. Just let it happen." He kissed my cheek in a way that was all too endearing for a man like him. "You feel incredible. I can *feel* how close you are."

"Ugh," I grunted in frustration. I was dehydrated, hungry, exhausted. No wonder I never used to care for morning sex.

"You sure you don't want me to touch you?"

"No, too sensitive."

"Here," he pressed on my back. "Roll over."

I rolled onto my stomach as the solid wall of his chest lifted away from my back. The next thing I felt was a playful smack on my ass.

"Keep them legs closed," he chuckled before pressing my hips down into the mattress.

When he started thrusting again, new sensations exploded within my body. Now the bed underneath me added indirect pressure to my clit, along with my thighs still squeezing together. His cock stroked inside me at a new, deeper angle. Instead of tiptoeing toward a release, I was now sprinting at full speed.

"Oh...God...fuck!" The moans and expletives left my mouth faster than my brain could catch up. I gripped the sheets in my fists and held on for dear life.

"That's my girl," Reaper groaned, his hips bouncing

off my ass with each tireless thrust. "Come all over my cock."

"I'm gonna...God...Reaper..."

While teetering on the edge, I felt his body lean over to hover above mine. His lips skimmed over my nape as he whispered, "Mariposa…"

I hurtled over the edge and shattered into a million pieces. Reaper pressed one final, deep stroke inside me before he let out a shuddering moan against my back. The spasms and convulsions did all the work for us, drawing my orgasm out longer while milking his release deep within me.

By the time my orgasm subsided, I had no energy to even lift my head and rest it on Reaper's chest.

"That did it," I mumbled into the twisted, rumpled sheets. "You didn't just break me. I'm dead."

"Death by orgasms," he laughed breathlessly, running a hand down my spine. "What a way to go."

MARIPOSA

I must have dozed off again, because Reaper's smack on my ass jolted me so hard I nearly hit the ceiling.

"Ugh, no. No more," I whined, covering myself with the sheet. "I need at least twelve hours before I can go again."

"Same here, sugar," he squeezed my shoulder as he kissed my neck. "It's coffee and breakfast time. For real, now."

I rolled over to find he was half-dressed and in the process of putting on a shirt. Giving him my sweetest, most alluring smile, I said, "Will you bring some up for me?"

"Hm," he pondered, stroking my cheek. "No."

"Ugh, what?"

The bastard had the nerve to laugh at my crestfallen face. "As much as I enjoy you," he pecked a kiss on my lips, "I'm not *that* pussy-whipped." He swatted my ass again before standing up. "Let's go."

I rolled out of bed and pulled on clothes while he

and Hades waited by the door. The dog's ears perked up at the sight of me, his paws tapping excitedly on the floor as I approached.

"Hey, boy! Let me see your wound."

I shouldn't have been surprised but my pulse sped up at the sight anyway. The incision was completely closed and the scar tissue faded to a pale grey color.

"Looks like I can cut off those stitches, boy." Then to Reaper, "I can't get over how weird this is. This doesn't freak you out at all?"

"Why would it?" He pulled open the door and led us out into the hallway. "If it means my best friend can survive what's thrown at him and it keeps him around longer, why would I question that?"

"Because it's scientifically impossible," I said. "Tissue can take weeks to reconnect. Not to mention all the blood vessels and the nerve damage from a cut that deep—"

"You're talking to a guy who never finished high school, Miss Medic," Reaper looked at me coyly. "And I was stoned for most of the time I was there. I don't know any of that scientific stuff you learned with a fancy education. All I know is what the world has shown me."

"Oh," I said blankly, taken aback. "Sorry, I didn't know."

"You didn't ask." He threw an arm over my shoulder as we descended the stairs, then pressed a kiss to my temple. "It's all right, sugar. The onset of the Collapse prevented a lot of us from seeking higher education."

"How so?" I glanced at his hand hanging over my

shoulder and wondered how weird it would be if I tried to hold it.

"Did you ever watch the news?" he teased. "The feds decimated school funding. Teachers' pay became a pittance. Nearly every public school in Arizona went on strike, which accomplished jack fucking shit. That was about five years pre big-C."

"I heard about the school protests all around the country then. But that was when the news channels in Texas started being cut off and we depended on random radio reports. We never knew what to believe."

"Which was exactly what they wanted," Reaper muttered.

"It just surprises me," I looked up at him, the stubble on his jaw getting longer in the past few days. "You lead a powerful MC, you ask so many questions, even about abstract ideas—"

"You saying I'm smarter than I look?" he grinned.

"I didn't mean it like that," I stammered. "You just don't *act* like you're uneducated."

"Something my father told me," his voice lowered after a few moments of silence, "was if someone claimed to have all the answers, they were full of shit. Question what they say, and see how their actions match their words." His arm lifted off my shoulders and I felt his fingers skim down my back. "Hades has always been loyal to me, so I'm less inclined to question every little thing that happens to him."

We made our way into the dining room as he spoke, his fellow Steel Demons milling about like regular hotel guests at a continental breakfast. Their eyes lifted to him as we passed, mumbling words of greeting to their president and none to me.

Of course not. Why would they? A sobering realization hit me out of nowhere. He might be sweet to me in the bedroom but out here, I was just Reaper's arm candy. His flavor of the week, or month if I was lucky. Aside from eye-fucking me at the Old Phoenix service center, his men barely acknowledged my existence.

It was painfully obvious as Reaper stopped to chat with two of Gunner's guardsmen. His hand drifted up to rub a gentle massage on the nape of my neck. I might as well have been carved from wood—nothing but a prop for him to touch and claim ownership of.

The longer I stood there, the more uncomfortable I became. Reaper must have noticed me stiffen because his fingers dug harder into my neck. I was moments away from slapping his hand off of me when I spotted Gunner striding down the long corridor ahead of us.

"Gunner!" I called to him with a wave and my heart lifted at his returned smile. Now there was a rare man who didn't see women as disposable sex dolls.

"Morning, Mari." Horus spread his wings and sailed off his shoulder to land on the breakfast bar next to us, much to the dismay of the guy Reaper was talking to.

Upon closer look, Gunner was dressed for riding. He has his tactical-style cut on, decked out with pockets and holders for weapons and ammo.

"Going for a ride?" I asked him.

His smile faded, lips pressing together into a thin line. "Yeah. I'd take you with, but I'm gonna be gone for a couple of weeks."

"What?" I cried.

"Fuckin' *excuse me*?" Reaper whirled around on him at the same time. "Care to explain where the fuck *this* came from, Captain?"

"President," Gunner returned stiffly. "Can I have a word?"

"Can you have a word, just fuck me with a cactus already..."

Reaper stormed off grumbling. Gunner shot me an apologetic look before following his president to a private spot near the outside walkway. Now alone, I went straight for the food, not caring to stand around awkwardly by Reaper's men.

I piled a plate full of scrambled eggs with sides of potatoes and prickly pear fruit, then went on a hunt for coffee. Apparently I wasn't the only one.

Shadow towered over the drink counter, emptying a large French press into an even larger mug that was probably meant for beer. I came up next to him, grabbing the last coffee press that still had coffee in it.

"Good morning, Shadow," I greeted as I poured.

He responded with a flinch and a grunt, then slamming his empty coffee press down as he walked away quickly.

I watched him move swiftly through the dining room for a man his size. He sat next to Jandro, who was talking to another one of Gunner's men.

His behavior didn't offend me. I knew he wouldn't respond with typical behavior and was curious to see what that would be. At some point, I wanted to learn what it took to hear him say one word to me. I didn't even know what his voice sounded like.

Horus had apparently annoyed the two guys at the breakfast bar enough to make them move, so I set myself up a few feet away from the falcon.

"Hi, Horus. Can I sit with you?"

He looked at me, tilting his head a bit, then looked at my food before taking a few cautious steps forward on those menacing talons.

"Guess that's a yes." I slid into the stool, careful not to make any sudden movements.

Hades was one thing, but I wasn't foolish enough to think I could treat this bird like a dog. Horus seemed to tolerate my presence at least, eyeing me intently as I brought a forkful of eggs to my mouth.

Within a minute he seemed to grow bored of me, fluffing up his feathers to preen himself.

Every so often I glanced from the bird to Gunner and Reaper, who seemed to be having an intense conversation next to a column. Abruptly, Reaper turned away with his hands in the air as if exasperated. He marched to the drink table, apparently in search of coffee. Gunner came straight toward me, an uneasy smile on his face.

"You're really leaving?" was the first thing I asked.

"Yeah, baby girl," he sighed, reaching out to stroke Horus's chest feathers. "I don't want to, but important business has come up."

"Why's Reaper so upset?" My eyes slid over to the president cursing and gesticulating over the lack of coffee.

"I didn't exactly ask him for permission to leave," Gunner smirked. "He doesn't like that I undermined his authority, but he knows how important this business is."

"Top secret club business?" I lifted an eyebrow.

"Kinda, but more than that," he said softly. "It's for everything we've worked for. It's making sure everyone back at Sheol is safe and secure."

"Sounds serious." I took in how armed he was. A gun at each hip, knives on his belt, bandoliers of ammo across his torso. And that was just what I could *see*. "And dangerous."

"Both of those statements are true."

Without thinking, I leaned forward and grabbed the edge of his cut, drawing him a few steps closer to me.

"Be careful," I whispered, suddenly feeling too bashful to look him in the eye. So I gazed at his lips. "I won't be out there to fix you up."

"Trust me, baby girl," he lifted my gaze with a finger under my chin, "whoever gets in my way is the one that needs to be careful."

My thumb brushed over the 2A patch on his cut. The now-dissolved right to bear arms was a philosophy he embodied deeply. I'd never seen him in action with a weapon so he was probably right. Every time I looked at the beautiful golden-haired, blue-eyed man, it was hard to reconcile such an angelic face with bloodlust and violence. For all I knew, he probably used it to his advantage.

"Just make sure you get back," I laughed awkwardly. "You have to keep me from drowning."

"I will." His hand remained on my face. "Horus will stay here. Think of him as me in bird form."

"He's not going with you?"

"Not this time. We need him to keep an eye on things here."

"What do you mean?"

His eyes flicked up to Reaper, who appeared to have found some coffee after all and was coming toward us with his own plate of food.

"I should get going. Take care, Mari. I—" His eyes flickered down, the bashful one for once. "I'll be thinking of you."

He dropped a kiss to my forehead and was gone, booted feet stomping across the floor to the garage in the next moment.

"So." Reaper dropped his plate with a loud clatter next to mine, clearly still in a bad mood. "We're stuck with you now, are we?"

He was talking to Horus, who replied with a high-pitched screech and a beat of his wings.

"Great. Thanks for the fucking feather in my eggs, bird."

I hid my chuckle behind a sip of coffee. "What did Gunner mean, that Horus is going to keep an eye on things?"

He stabbed the feathered chunk of scrambled eggs and dropped it onto a napkin before answering. "Horus is a bird of prey. They have binocular vision and can see fine details from hundreds of yards away."

"Okay...?"

"And what he sees, Gunner sees."

"Come again?"

Reaper grinned deviously. "I thought you needed time off from me, sugar."

"Stop." I smacked his hand that began creeping up my thigh. "What do you mean, Gunner sees what Horus sees?"

"It's like a live video feed through those webcams. You remember those?" He swiped a tortilla from the warmer nearby and proceeded to fill it with scrambled egg and potatoes.

"You're fucking with me, right?" I stared blankly as he made a breakfast taco.

"No, I'm not." He dumped hot sauce into his taco and took a big bite.

"Reaper, this is like what I was saying earlier," I lowered my voice to a whisper, although I wasn't sure why. "That's not possible. It's completely and absolutely *im*-possible."

"Clearly not, miss fancy degree."

"Do you and Hades have that same kind of...thing?"

He chewed methodically before swallowing his food. "No. We have a bond, but I can't see through him like Gunner does with Horus."

"Reaper." My mind spun at a rate I couldn't keep up with. I felt like my head was going to implode on itself. "You realize this is *not* normal, right? Like, this is the most absurd shit I've ever heard of."

He laughed calmly as he made another breakfast taco. "Ain't nothing normal about the world we live in, sugar."

EIGHT

JANDRO

I watched Mari and Reaper walk in late to the dining room with curiosity. She had that beautiful post-sex glow, and he swaggered in like a peacock.

And with good reason. He was the only Demon getting laid out here.

I never was a jealous guy. I knew my place well enough that I'd never undermine my president's and best friend's claim on a woman. If he was down to share her, I'd jump at the first chance. But it had to be his call.

Because of how Reaper was raised, bringing another man in was serious and meaningful. Which was the opposite of how most people saw group situations—as meaningless fun. The officials who raided the matriarchal communes claimed they were cleaning out dens of sin and unholiness. I preferred to think they were just jealous, frustrated virgins.

In any case, Reaper and I never shared a woman before because he never found anyone he cared enough about. He and I were close, but I didn't grow up in the communes. So I could see it both ways. I certainly had my fair share of casual group fun, but wouldn't mind doing it with a serious partner in the right setting.

Reaper was crazy about Mari, and it was plainly obvious to anyone who looked. He never stopped touching her, whether his arm was around her shoulders or on the small of her back. He'd broach the topic of sharing soon, if he hadn't already. And then it was still up to her to accept it. Not all of the matriarchal women accepted multiple partners.

But if she *did*, I wanted a shot at being her second man.

Just the thought of calling her mine sent a flutter of warmth through me. Maybe it was presumptive—we hadn't gotten to know each other *that* well yet. But I was drawn to her warm, caring nature like a moth to a flame. So many free women became tough and cutthroat after the Collapse. They had to be, to not be ruled under the thumb of men. But even with her sassy mouth and dirty scrubs, Mariposa had a soft, feminine nature in her that called to the traditional family man in me.

As Gunner walked down the corridor and came brazenly straight toward her, *that* was when the first spark of jealousy lit up within me.

We may have had a friendly, unspoken competition going, in regards to having her on our bikes, but he had no right to walk right up like she was *his* girl.

I knew it, and apparently Reaper knew it by the way he glared at the blue-eyed demon. To be fair, Gunner had no idea how relationships worked in the matriarchies. He grew up wealthy, the descendant of Hollywood actors who moved east as California began to sink into the ocean they poisoned. One rumor claimed his family had ties to the politicians who set the Collapse in motion, though he always vehemently denied it.

But what pissed me off the most was how Mari looked at him, smiling like the sun shined out of his ass. I had no one to blame but myself for staying out of the way, but what utter bullshit was that?

When Gunner and Reaper walked off to exchange heated words, I wanted to trade my scrambled eggs for a bowl of popcorn. What the hell was that about? Reaper said he trusted the guy.

Shadow sat down heavily next to me as I was pondering all this. He dug ruthlessly into his eggs as if the chicken had personally insulted him.

"She said *good morning* to me," he grumbled.

"Yeah, and?" I couldn't prevent my shoulders shaking from laughter. "Did you say anything back?"

"No! You know I don't talk to women."

"Bro," I rubbed my forehead with a sigh. "Just talking to them isn't gonna hurt you. You could afford to learn some social skills."

"I don't like being social."

"Neither do lots of people," I said. "But sometimes you run into situations where you have to do it anyway."

He wordlessly grunted as he dug into his breakfast. We had this conversation many times before.

"Tell me something," I said, watching Mari grab a seat at the breakfast bar next to Horus. "You've truly never said a word to the service girls I've sent you?"

"No," he answered after a swig of coffee. "They come to me, do what they're paid for, and they leave."

"Seriously, no cuddling afterward?" I asked. "No pillow talk?"

"I don't even know what those things are." He blinked at me, only his dark eye visible with the white one covered by his hair. "Why would a woman spend time with me beyond what she's paid for?"

"I mean, that's part of it sometimes, you know? Intimacy, closeness. At least the illusion of it. Everyone needs a little human connection."

He shook his head as if I were spouting nonsense. "I don't need anything from a woman. I keep telling you bartering with service girls for me is a waste of resources."

"You're telling me you can go without sex?" I demanded in disbelief. "For the rest of your life?"

"I can think back to my favorites and use my hand."

Anyone else would have been joking, but Shadow never joked.

"Unbelievable," I groaned. "Sometimes I wonder why I even try with you."

"You have stuck by me for years," he acquiesced. "And helped me in many ways. But I'm sure you knew when you first saw me that I would never be a 'normal' person."

"No one is normal, bro. I don't care what anyone says. Hey, tell me something," I turned to him. "How do you decide on a favorite?"

"You mean of women who've serviced me?"

"Yeah. You like blondes, brunettes? Thick and curvy

or slim and petite? Maybe we can just find you more of whatever you like."

His gaze lifted across the dining hall, settling on the only woman in the room. Mariposa had her back to us, long brown hair cascading over her shoulders as she sat with Reaper at the breakfast bar.

"My favorites are the ones who are good at pretending they're not afraid of me," Shadow answered softly.

NINE

MARIPOSA

No matter how much he tried to brush it off, I couldn't stop asking Reaper questions about what he called his *bond* with Hades.

The nurse in me wanted to examine it like an ailment. Or I guess it was more like an ability. Maybe even a super-power.

"Can you describe the bond with Hades?" I asked as we walked through the outpost after breakfast. "Have you felt it with any other animal?"

"Never." He lit a slim black cigarette and turned his head so the smoke wouldn't blow my way. "I've always been shitty with animals. I accidentally killed Noelle's pet fish when we were kids."

"Wow. She must have hated you." An unexpected pang hit me in the chest. I missed my friend, Reaper's sister, back at Sheol. I wasn't about to make friends with the kitchen girls and I felt a twinge of loneliness without another woman to talk to. If nothing else, she might be able to decipher her brother's behavior for me. I still felt so clueless about MC life and what roles women played.

"Oh yeah. She gave me a black eye and didn't talk to me for a week," he chuckled. "But Hades was different the moment I found him. Even before I found him, I had this...feeling. It sounds girly as shit, but I don't know how else to describe it."

"What kind of feeling?"

He gave me a sideways glance. "You're really not gonna let this go, are you?"

"I'm still astonished you haven't tried to pick this apart to understand it. I don't know how you just accept it as it is."

"Because it's always felt *right*," he answered after exhaling smoke. "Something nagged at me for a whole fucking day to check this pile of rubble. And when I did, and I found this tiny puppy who fit in the palm of my hand, I just *knew* I found what I'd been looking for."

He looked ahead to where Hades, now fully grown, trotted a few paces in front of us. He occasionally sniffed the ground, pissed on a bush, and looked back at us as if to make sure we were still following.

"I felt like I was *meant* to find Hades," Reaper continued softly. "Like we were always supposed to be together. I was meant to raise him and he was meant to look after me." He tossed his cigarette butt and added in an even softer voice, "And those closest to me."

"And you've done that for each other," I observed. "Since day one."

"If I had ignored that feeling back then," Reaper shook his head. "He wouldn't have lived. I'm sure of it. I saved his life and he's saved mine countless times in return. And it's only been a year."

"You two are closer than most humans are to each other. You're almost like brothers."

"Yeah." My pulse hammered as Reaper's hand bumped into mine and he grabbed it, lacing his fingers with mine. "I haven't really talked about this with anyone but Gunner, whose experience with Horus is similar but different. And Jandro and Noelle, who know everything about me. Most of the club thinks I'm just an expert dog trainer or some shit."

"See?" I dared to give his fingers a playful squeeze. "You do know this is unusual, otherwise you'd have no qualms talking about your...gift."

"Ain't 'cause of that, sugar," he chuckled. "I just know what it sounds like—feminine mumbo jumbo. Being sensitive to energies and shit. They wouldn't understand."

"I don't understand," I admitted, watching Hades stiffen and growl at a lizard. "But I'm trying to."

"I knew you would," he murmured.

"What made you pick the name Hades?" The dog in question grew bored with the lizard and moved on to sniffing in a lazy zig-zag. "Were you interested in Greek mythology?"

"I didn't pick it," Reaper said. "That was his name."

"Oh, you mean he had a collar on when you found him?"

"No, that was just *his* name. It came to me in my head but I didn't choose it, if that makes sense."

I stopped in my tracks, pulling him back by his hand when he tried to keep walking.

"That makes zero sense. You're actually fucking with me now, aren't you?"

"I swear I never heard the word Hades in my life before then," he insisted. "It was like," he paused to watch his dog chase after a bird, "like he *told* me his name."

"The more you tell me about this, the more fucking confused I get," I groaned, rubbing my temple.

"See? Better to not think about it so much," he teased, pulling me by the hand to keep walking.

The momentum sent me crashing into his side, which he used as an opportunity to drape his arm over my shoulders and kiss my temple. I slid an arm around his waist to coolly match his affection, but that didn't quell my insides shooting off like fireworks.

Fuck, fuck, fuck. I thought I could do casual sex but I really had to get my feelings in check. Chances were higher that he'd discard me than keep me, and I had to prepare myself for that. Which meant not reading into the hand-holding. Or the kissing. Or his flirting and playful banter. Nor his insistence on making me come no less than a dozen times in a night. That was probably just his kink.

"I don't know who or what exactly Hades is," he mused, oblivious to the turmoil of my inner thoughts. "But I'm glad he's on our side."

"Where did Gunner ride off to?" I asked, ready for a subject change.

"To take care of club business," he answered dismissively. "He goes off solo to secure deals sometimes."

"He made it sound like it was something big and out of the ordinary." I gave Reaper a jab in the ribs. "And that you were pissed because he didn't ask you first."

"Woman, you are too fucking observant and curious for your own good." He lowered his forehead to mine and dropped a kiss on my nose with a smile. "It's a good thing I trust you."

"So," I looked up, the sun and bleached desert landscape making his eyes shine like two emeralds, "what's going on?"

"We're dealing with something here," he sighed, "that requires all hands on deck. With him gone, it leaves me short-handed. And without going into specifics, him leaving with no warning looks bad to the club. But he is taking care of something of utmost importance so I had to let him go, as much as I don't like it."

We walked a few more paces. Hades rolled onto his back, twisting and squirming with his tongue hanging out the side of his mouth like a goofball.

"Anything I can do?" I asked after a few quiet moments.

"Aren't you sweet, sugar." He squeezed the nape of my neck. "Tensions are high, so the guys might take a few swings at each other. If they get seriously hurt, don't let them kill each other."

"That I can do," I smiled. "Anything else?"

His hand slid down to cup the small of my back.

"Scream my name when I'm inside you." His

whisper was hot against my ear. "Come all over my cock like you'll never let it go. Sleep with your head on my chest and let me massage your worries away. Rub my balls—"

"Okay!" I laughed, shoving him away. "Jesus, I never know when you're going to be dirty or romantic."

"Gotta keep you on your toes." He pulled me into his side again with another devilish grin. "He likes you, you know."

"Who?"

"You know," he chided gently. "Gunner."

And I like him. Like hell I would say that out loud to Reaper of all people.

Of all these men, Gunner was the one I considered most like a friend. He was all smiles and lightheartedness, a pleasant distraction from his broody cohorts. His presence was like the sun's warmth, and not just because he was golden and gorgeous. If anyone else tried teaching me to not drown, I probably would not have been as calm. I was really sad to find out he'd be gone for several weeks. Not that I didn't enjoy being around Reaper or Jandro, but *friend* was not the first word that came to mind when I thought of them.

"He's a flirt," I said in response to Reaper's statement. "I'm sure he acts the way he does around all women, but I do consider him a friend."

"A friend," he repeated. "Nothing more?"

I looked up at him to find his gaze on Hades' antics once again. "Are you trying to insinuate something?"

"Not at all, just trying to gauge how you feel about him."

"He's a friend," I repeated. *That I'm really fucking attracted to.* "I trust him," I added.

"Jandro likes you, too," he chuckled with a squeeze of my waist.

"He's an even bigger flirt," I rolled my eyes. "But I don't know him as well. Gunner and I have actually talked a bit more."

"Ah. Well now with Gunner gone, you might have time to make *friends* with Jandro, too."

I stared at his side profile—the scruffy jawline, sharp cheekbones, and the straight bridge of his nose. But he kept looking at the path straight ahead of us.

"Why do I feel like you're implying something without coming out and saying it?" I asked. "Like you're trying to pass me off to your friends or something."

"I'm not." He stopped us, turning to face me with his arms locked around my waist. "It's not like that, sugar. I just—" He looked down, fingers gliding across my ribcage. If I had to guess, he looked nervous.

"I just want you to get to know my friends," he said. "As a way of getting to know me. They're like family to me."

"So," I tilted my head, still not buying it. "You want me to get closer to your family? By teasing me about your two most flirtatious men?"

"It came out wrong," he sighed, releasing his hold on me as he continued walking. "Forget I said anything."

"Reaper." I jogged after him to catch up. "I'm *trying* to understand you. All this is just a lot to take in—"

"I know, that's my bad." He shot me a sheepish

smile. "One thing at a time. My crazy bond with my dog is enough for one day, don't you think?"

"Okay," I said, running a hand through my hair. "So what are you up to today?"

"Church for a second try," he grumbled, fishing for another cigarette. "Let's see if we can have a successful meeting without Gunner's hotheaded ass."

I had a hard time picturing my calm, reassuring swim coach as hotheaded. Something really had to be sowing discord within the club to get under his skin.

"Okay," I repeated, honestly grateful for some space from Reaper today. I needed alone time to digest everything he told me about the animal bonds, and his men. And to wrestle with my feelings for this man, growing like stubborn weeds through cracks in a sidewalk.

He slid both hands to my ass, drawing me flush against him and holding me there with his green gaze.

"See you tonight." It wasn't a request. "You know where to be."

He claimed my mouth in a bruising kiss while I held onto my sanity like a life raft, trying not to get swept away in the undertow.

But this demon was riding his way directly into my heart, and I was powerless to stop him.

REAPER

"How's *Marrriposa?*"

Jandro and Shadow were the first two in the conference room. Already there when I arrived, the former had his boots up on the table. The latter sat strategically near the head of the table where he could see the whole room. Typical Shadow.

"She's great. Ruined," I smirked. "How are the bikes?"

"We'll be fine to head back, but they're gonna need some tuning once I get 'em back in the shop," Jandro shook his head. "The elevation and terrain aren't good up here, Reap. This is what I was saying before."

"We're no longer doing business with Tash now, so it's a moot point," I said, looking up at the rafters. "I wouldn't mind keeping this place for us, though. It's nice, well-supplied, and Fischlin's just abandoned it."

"He could come back with reinforcements," Shadow pointed out. "General Tash must know we haven't been captured or killed by now. He'll send well-armed rein-forcements."

"Armed thanks to us," Jandro muttered.

"I did think of that, Shadow," I nodded. "This is a good outpost, although we're isolated here and not familiar with the terrain. When everyone gets here, I'm going to propose we ride back home tomorrow."

"Yes!" Jandro shot his fists in the air. "Can we take some chickens?"

"You gonna raise 'em in your backyard?" I scoffed.

"I dunno, maybe."

"I'm not dealing with any crowing at the ass-crack of dawn," I growled, taking my seat at the head of the table.

"Come on, Reap. You never know, maybe it's my calling to be a chicken rancher."

"I don't think that's what it's called," Shadow frowned.

"Gunner has a falcon. Maybe I was destined to have a chicken!"

"Enough already," I rubbed my forehead as everyone else started filing in.

My men took their seats, I hit the gavel and got right down to business.

"If you fuckers can act like adults this time," I glow-ered, "we'll begin the meeting."

"Hey, you all saw it was Gunner that came after me," Big G announced. "Not saying that's an admission of guilt, but—"

"Don't. Fucking. Start." Jandro pointed a finger at

him in warning. "You provoked him. Any one of us would have acted the same way. I suggest you keep your mouth shut during this session, G."

The big fucker glared at his vice president but smartly held his tongue.

"General Tash, now a sworn enemy of ours," I began, "has likely heard by now that we've escaped capture and taken the outpost for ourselves. We have a well-stocked armory, but there are only seven of us. Plus two animals and one medic. It's fair to assume he'll return with a *much* bigger army to wipe us out for good. So I propose we ride back to Sheol in the morning, and figure out how to stick the two-timing shit bag from the safety of our own walls."

"Agreed," Jandro piped up right away. "All in favor?"

Every man at the table raised a hand.

"Good. It's settled." I struck the gavel on the table. "Start packing after dinner tonight and we'll ride at dawn. Next order of business." I set the gavel down and placed my palms on the table. "We have no need to kill Fischlin's snitch. So where do we drop him off?"

"Just leave him here," Big G scoffed. "Let Tash deal with him."

"Killing him will be the first thing they do," Brick pointed out.

"So? It ain't our problem."

"He's the reason we *know* Tash turned on us!"

Big G just shrugged and leaned back in his seat. A loyal guy and a good shot, he just didn't think very far ahead.

"President, if I may speak," Dallas piped up.

"Go ahead," I nodded.

He paused, tenting his fingers for a moment before speaking.

"I've probably spent more time with our prisoner than anyone else," he began. "He didn't turn on Fischlin because he's a little bitch. He *wants* to be a Steel Demon."

"Get the fuck outta here," Jandro cackled so hard, he nearly fell out of his chair.

"He has since we started building a reputation," Dallas went on. "Tash swept through his county like a wildfire just weeks after the Collapse. They massacred tons of innocents. His pregnant girlfriend died. He's wanted to take Tash down ever since."

"That's a nice sob story," I said. "Too bad everybody's got one. Losing everything to the Collapse sure as shit doesn't make you a Demon."

"He can ride," Dallas went on. "He used to build custom Harleys. Used to bow hunt for sport, so he's a good shot *and* can score us meat for the winter probably."

"I could use an extra hand in the shop," Jandro mused. "Especially after this trek home."

"*You're* getting on board with this?" I looked at my VP in disbelief. "You already have the fucking prospect!"

"I have to *teach* the prospect. I could use someone who actually knows what they're doing."

"Well, since you've gotten to be such good bosom buddies, tell me this," I crossed my arms, "is he loyal? Is he a man of his word? Will he ride with us to the center of Hell if I tell him to? Because *someone* who has sworn their loyalty, who I consider a brother, tried to get us all fucking killed!"

My fist slammed into the tabletop, creating a split in the flimsy wood. No one hardly dared to breathe as I shook my hand out.

"Who wants to keep the snitch in the club?" I growled through my teeth.

Jandro, Dallas, Brick, and Shadow raised their hands.

"You?" I looked at the large, silent man in surprise. "*You* trust the prisoner?"

"I'm not the best judge of people, but he seems genuine to me," Shadow answered. "If Jandro trusts him, then I do as well."

"All right, then." I looked at non-approving members. "We take him on as another prospect. He's not privy to church, patches, or any other privileges until Jandro and I both deem him worthy. Fair?"

A murmur of agreement rose from around the table. Satisfied, I struck the gavel.

"Any other club business to attend to?"

"Can we just come out and say it instead of dancing around the subject?" Big G asked.

I narrowed my eyes. "What are you referring to?"

"Did you not hear me about keeping your mouth shut?" Jandro leaned over the table like he wanted to cross over and strangle him.

"Gunner is the one who sold us out to Tash. Isn't it obvious to anyone else?" Big G looked around the table, apparently for rallying cries of support but was met with silence.

"Gunner is *our* brother. *Your* captain, until he rightfully kicked you out," Jandro seethed. "Why do you have such a hard-on for throwing him to the wolves?"

"Why can't *you* see what's right in front of you?" Big G shot back. "He's the only one in regular contact with Tash. He's got all these mysterious black market connections outside the club, and now he's just taken off to fuck knows where!"

"He's headed to the Colorado territory to work out new deals," I said. "Because Sheol depends on him and he's the only one who can make that happen."

"Sure, that's what he told *you*, Reaper."

"Do not take me for a fool," I warned him, my hands closing into fists. "I'm still your president, whether you agree with my decisions or not."

"You didn't answer my question," Jandro jumped to his feet, rounding the table toward the loudmouth. "Why are you so quick to be pointing fingers? You got something to hide?"

"Like what?" G brought his palms down on the table as he stood up. "I'm fucking loyal! I ain't hiding shit!"

"Everyone out," I barked, slamming the gavel down as I stood up. "Except you, G."

Jandro didn't move an inch, his shoulders squared and tense as a brick wall.

"You want to question your president's leadership and sow distrust, you're in the wrong fucking club." Even as he defended me, Jandro seemed to forget I was there, even when I brought a hand down on his shoulder.

"Easy, VP." I moved to stand at his side, arms crossed against my chest as we stared down Big G together. "You're not leaving this room until you tell us what your fucking agenda is."

"The fuck?" His mouth dropped open. "My only agenda is outing the son-of-a-bitch who sold us out!"

"It's not Gunner," Jandro hissed through his teeth. "We would know. So get that notion out of your head before we beat it out of you."

"Yeah?" G stepped closer into Jandro's face. "So your word is the law now, J? Even without any proof?"

"You don't have a shred of proof either, you dumb fuck!"

Big G pulled back his arm to swing. I stepped between him and Jandro but despite being right there, I still wasn't as fast as Shadow.

The silent assassin got behind Big G somehow, grabbing hold of his wrist to prevent him from slugging the vice president.

"Let go of me, freak!" G tried to wrench his arm away but Shadow was five steps ahead, holding strong while pulling him away from Jandro.

"I don't want to hurt you, Big G," Shadow said with an eerie calm. "But you're not thinking of the consequences if you lay a hand on Jandro."

Even without Shadow and Jandro being extra protective of each other, physical altercations were forbidden except during Fight Night. I had a feeling

Jandro, Big G, and possibly Gunner would have some serious beef to settle at an upcoming fight.

"You're fucking lucky Shadow stopped you," I growled at Big G. "Attacking your vice president gets that patch ripped right off your cut in front of the whole club. Is *that* what you're trying to do here? Get yourself kicked out?"

"No." Big G deflated and Shadow cautiously released his arm, as he looked like he was finally coming to his senses. "Sorry, guys. I'm just trying to do the right thing. I hate that there's a snake among us, you know? It just feels so obvious that it's Gunner—"

"Even if it is," I interrupted. "This is not the right way to go about it. Talk to us like a man, don't throw tantrums like a child when you don't get your way."

"You're right, Reap. Of course." He forced out a dry laugh. "I got two kids with a third on the way. I should know better. Maybe the stress of a new kid is getting to me, I don't know."

"Well, get it together," Jandro snapped. "We don't need the club falling apart because of accusations and rumors. We *will* find who turned on us, and deal with him accordingly."

"In the meantime," I scratched the stubble on my jaw. "I think a slow cook will be a fitting punishment for you."

Big G opened his mouth to complain, then smartly closed it. "How long?" he asked in a small voice.

"The whole way home. You wanted to be a rabble rouser and bathe in the club's attention, now you'll get to."

Jandro stifled a chuckle as Big G hung his head.

"Thank you, President," came his humiliated reply.

"Think before you speak next time, chief." I slapped his shoulder and looked at my other two men. "We done here?"

We closed up the room and Big G hurried off toward the kitchen, likely to drink himself stupid in light of his punishment tomorrow.

"Go ahead and start getting packed," Jandro said to Shadow. "I'll meet you in the dining hall later."

With a curt nod, Shadow turned sharply down a corridor and disappeared without making a sound.

"So," Jandro said the moment we were alone. "You think it's G?"

I pulled out my cigarettes and handed one to him. "Nah." My inhale was sharp as I pulled my first drag. "He's not the sharpest tool in the shed, but he's loyal."

"Same." Jandro blew out a long exhale. "He's been wanting captain of the guard for a while now. Probably saw it as an opportunity for Gun's post and a chance for a little time in the spotlight."

"Please," I scoffed. "He is nowhere near qualified to take captain. I'd give it to Shadow before him."

"Dude wants to feel important," Jandro shrugged. "We're on the road so much, Tessa pretty much raises their kids and runs the home alone. She doesn't need him."

"You think she's caught on to him messing around?" I asked. "Maybe he's trying to overcompensate his usefulness."

"I dunno, man," Jandro raised both hands, "I'm not in their business much. I try to stay out of it. All I know is he's been trying to move up the ranks."

"Then he needs to fucking act like it." I tossed my cigarette butt over the balcony and headed for my suite.

MARIPOSA

"Mari?"

"In here."

I was soaking in Reaper's bathtub when his loud, booted footsteps echoed through the suite. Hades ran to me, stubby tail wagging like he hadn't seen me in years.

"Hi, boy. Oh—okay!" I squeezed my eyes shut against the onslaught of licks to my face.

Reaper came into the bathroom a few seconds later, watching us with a lazy smirk.

"I was hoping to get some use out of that thing before we leave." He peeled off his shirt, discarding it on the floor before kicking off his boots.

"This tub's much nicer than the one in my room," I smiled back. "We leaving soon?"

"Tomorrow morning." He unzipped his pants and shoved them down his thighs, peeling them away until he was just standing there in his birthday suit.

My throat constricted just slightly, although I had no idea why. I'd seen him naked before, much closer than this, and touched just about every part of him that I could see.

"Quit drooling and move over, sugar." He came to the tub's edge and ran his fingers over the surface, splashing me with a grin.

"I was *not* drooling," I muttered, yanking my eyes away as I scooted to make room for him.

"Sure you weren't." He lowered himself into the steaming water with a sigh. "Now come here."

I moved back to the spot in front of him, where his arms opened. The water had a thin layer of pinkish foam from the bath bomb I used. So while the water was partially opaque, I still felt apprehensive and exposed. I'd had sex with this man half a dozen times at this point. Why did a bath feel so much more intimate?

The feeling intensified as he turned me around gently and pulled me toward him until my back touched his chest. I sat between his legs, which nearly extended the entire length of the luxurious porcelain tub. He let out a contented sigh when I relaxed against him, pressing a kiss to my ear as his fingers massaged into my arms and shoulders.

Jesus. It was like *he* couldn't relax until he was making *me* feel good.

That was a dangerous train of thought, and one I'd been trying to talk myself out of all day. I must have walked through every corridor of this outpost today while my mind went in circles about him. I could *not* afford to develop feelings for the Steel Demons president, and I was a damned fool to even entertain the thought he had feelings for me.

But from the way my insides fluttered as his touch drifted over my skin, I had a sinking feeling it was too late for me.

"How was church?" I asked, focusing on a random bubble on the water's surface.

"Marginally more productive than yesterday," he grunted. "We're taking Fischlin's guard home with us."

"Really?" I looked at him over my shoulder, genuinely surprised. "What made you change your mind?"

"Jandro and Dallas made pretty convincing arguments."

"Uh huh. And who put the idea in your head first?"

"Don't get cocky, woman," he laughed. "You're starting to sound like one of us."

"It was just a matter of time, I guess."

"Mm." He pressed a kiss to my cheek before slowly moving his lips down my neck. All the while, his thumbs pressed slow circles into my upper back.

"Why do you do this?" I groaned, letting my head fall back.

"Do what?" he chuckled, knowing full well what he was doing.

"Massage me. Get me off until my clit is completely numb before getting yours. It just seems like a lot of...effort."

"I like making you feel good." Another smoldering kiss dropped between my neck and shoulder. "I think you're worth the effort."

"Don't tell me things like that," I snapped, a knee-jerk reaction.

"Then don't ask questions like those." He nipped at my neck and it was frustrating how good that felt, too.

"Fine. Forget I said anything."

"Mm, can't put that genie back in the bottle now, sugar." He rested his chin on my shoulder as his arms circled around my waist. "Just imagine if there were two or three of me," he added in a sultry whisper.

"What?"

"Four hands massaging you." He began kneading my thighs under the water's surface. "Two mouths kissing all your little hot spots so we don't miss a single one. Roughness and sweetness at the same time. Would you like that?"

"Reaper," I lifted myself away and turned around to face him. "What are you talking about?"

"Pleasing you even more," his voice was thick with desire, "by bringing in another man."

"I don't want another man." The words came out before I could think, and I bit my tongue too late. It wasn't a true confession of anything, but still felt like it all the same.

Reaper cocked an eyebrow. "I don't know if that's entirely true." His fingers skimmed through the water, reaching for my hands. "It's okay, Mari. If you're into one or two of my men, I can work with that."

"What the hell?" I pulled further away, confusion twisting in my gut. "Do you do this with every woman?"

"No." Then softer, "I've *never* done this before." He sighed deeply and ran his fingers through his hair, making water droplets rain down on his face and shoulders. "And I'm doing a bang-up fucking job, it seems."

"You want to pass me around to your men like a pitcher of beer for what, exactly? So you can have free rein to fuck other women?"

"Fucking Christ, Mari. When have I *ever* said shit about other women? That's not what this is about."

"If you were done with me, you could have just said so." I dug myself into a hole and apparently insisted on digging even deeper. I was being ridiculous, pulling assumptions out of thin air most likely. But it dawned on me I could finally do what escaped me the last few days.

Protect my heart.

"You've got it all wrong, sugar. But fine, have it your way." He leaned back, propping one elbow on the edge of the tub as he looked out the window. "Leave."

I blinked, taken aback by the sudden change in attitude. "What?"

"You want us to be done? Fine. We're done. Get the hell out of my tub."

"I didn't say—"

"Get. Out." He looked at me with pure venom. "Before I do something I regret."

I stood up and stumbled so quickly out of the tub, it was a miracle I didn't slip and fall. Gathering up my clothes, I stole a glance at Hades with his head on his paws and ears back. He looked at me with such sadness with those big soulful eyes. I wanted to give him one last hug for comfort, but didn't dare.

I walked out of the bathroom, feeling crushed under Reaper's hurtful stare, with my clothes bundled against my chest. With shaking hands I got dressed in the bedroom as fast as I could. A high-pitched whine came from the bathroom.

"Hades, stay," Reaper commanded.

So this *was* the end. He wouldn't even allow me a goodbye with the dog. For some reason, that cut deeper than him telling me to leave.

I hurried out as quickly as my feet could carry me, not caring that my clothes were now wet and I dripped water everywhere. This room was going to suffocate me if I didn't get out.

"Mariposa."

I froze in my tracks. "What?"

"Leave the door open for the next girl," Reaper called out cruelly.

I placed my hand on the doorknob, gripping it so hard that my palm ached. A white-hot flash of anger brought a moment of clarity to the confusion swirling around in my head. *Fuck him if he thinks he can still tell me what to do.*

I opened the door and slammed it shut with all my might behind me.

The tears started before I made it to my own room. I hurriedly unlocked the door through blurry eyes and entered a room that felt like someone else's.

I did what I had to. He would've broken my heart so much worse if I hadn't. It was shitty, but I had to put self-preservation first. That was what post-Collapse life demanded. I provoked a response out of him to protect myself.

So why did my heart still feel broken into a million pieces?

GUNNER

As much as I loved riding with my club, a solo ride had a certain kind of magic to it. There was nothing like exploring the world on the open road set out before me. I was the captain of my own ship, the president of Club Me, Myself, and I. The only thing that could beat this was if a beautiful woman hung onto me from behind.

And not just any woman.

Mariposa's face when I said I was leaving still tugged at my heart strings from two hundred miles away. If she tugged any harder, I might turn around and head right back to her.

Reaper better be good to you, baby girl, I thought, tightening my hold on my grips.

I had the utmost respect for my president and would defend his life in an instant. We were good friends, brothers, even. However, we had vastly different views on women.

While my parents worked, my grandparents watched

me and taught me old-school values as I grew up. For instance, even if a woman had a good career, the man always paid for dates and treated her with small surprise gifts like jewelry or flowers. He opened doors and pulled out chairs for her. He gave her his jacket off his back if she got cold. Women were smaller, more fragile, and meant to be taken care of. A man's job was to provide her with security and protection.

It took me a while to wrap my head around Reaper's whole matriarchy upbringing, and I still didn't fully understand. To be honest, it sounded like a cult to me. In my world, some women you had fun with, others you married, but his culture threw that all out the window. Women with multiple husbands? How could anyone be okay with that?

My grandparents were together for over fifty years and were each other's worlds. How could a relationship feel special if it was crowded with a bunch of people? Why would a woman miss you if she had other guys to fill up her time?

So much I didn't understand. But if that was what Mari wanted, too, I'd wish her the best and keep my distance.

When I stopped for a piss break, I let my eyes close and my awareness sink into what I called my second-consciousness. It wasn't my subconscious but a place deep and instinctual, underneath the layers of my human awareness and tucked away in the depths of my lizard brain.

At least I thought so. I wasn't sure exactly how it worked. All I knew was that it was my connection to

Horus, and it gave me the ability to see and feel everything he did like I was in his body.

"Gross, man," I muttered.

I checked in at a bad time, as Horus was currently ripping apart a rabbit carcass with his beak. But through the mess of blood, guts, and fur just under his talons, the Sandia Mountain outpost laid out before him.

It was quiet and without much movement, which didn't surprise me. The place was huge and sprawling with over a hundred guest rooms, each with mountain views, and we only took up nine of those rooms.

Well, eight if Mari was sharing a room with Reaper now.

As if he could hear my thought, Horus let out a disappointed squawk.

"Where is she?" I asked.

My raptor tore off another hunk of rabbit and swallowed it whole before turning his gaze to the southeast. He let out a soft chirp as if to say, *there*.

A small pen of animals was tucked between the kitchen and a steep hill. There was no clear outside path to it, only a single door on the building which I assumed to be the back door of the kitchen.

So that's where the chicken and eggs came from, I realized.

About twenty chickens milled about the pen—pecking, clucking, doing their chicken thing. Mari was scratching a goat behind the ears and smiling.

I finished pissing a whole few minutes ago, but didn't want to stop watching her. Still, I pulled my awareness away from Horus and back into my own body. With a sigh, I tucked myself back into my pants and zipped up. I had more of an already long ride ahead of me.

The terrain and atmosphere gradually changed the further north I rode. Dry, dusty desert grew rockier with cool, dark earth and more greenery alongside the road. The thick, hot air grew thinner and cooler as I climbed in elevation. Cactus and desert shrubs gave way to trees that grew steadily taller. When the early afternoon sun became dappled by the forest I rode through, I knew I reached the Colorado territory.

Or whatever it was named now. If I went looking, I could probably find the old "Welcome to Colorado" highway sign—covered in rust and filled with bullet holes, most likely.

A twinge of uneasiness hit me. I was technically in enemy territory. Well-armed, but alone. What most of the club didn't know was just how badly Tash's betrayal put us in a bind. Not that it was a secret, most of them just didn't understand the logistics of a carefully balanced economy. It was all gone to Hell now and only I could risk my neck to put it back together.

And shitheads like Big G wanted to throw baseless accusations and point fingers. Fuck him. He had no idea what I gave up to be a Steel Demon. If I wanted an easy life I could've easily had it, even after the world went to hell in a handbasket.

I cut ties with most people I knew before MC life. The majority of which I wouldn't hesitate to shoot if I saw them on the street. But I still had one big favor to cash in.

It was a long shot in the very best of circumstances.

Reaper had smoke coming out of his ears when I told him at breakfast, but he knew it was our best chance. Even though I brought it up, I almost wished he ordered me *not* to ride out so I wouldn't have to face this person.

Because there was a slim chance I might not make it back.

If this did work, though, we'd have the club well-provided for and Tash taken care of in one fell swoop. And that was worth the risk.

In a week, maybe less, I hoped to ride home with good news.

Colorado looked practically untouched by the Collapse as I rode through. Charming ranch homes on large plots of land decorated with aspen, pine, and oak trees dotted the mountainous landscape. I loved a scenic drive as much as the next person, but the ominous dread in my stomach over what awaited at my destination kept me from fully enjoying the view.

The sensation only grew, like a black hole in my body, as I turned off the highway to a hidden winding road. Anyone else would've missed it if they didn't know what to look for, but I knew too well.

The road was freshly paved and smooth on my tires, unheard of in the last decade unless you had enough wealth and power to afford it. Trees shading the road gave way abruptly to hills covered in vineyards. Rows upon rows of grapes created a repeating pattern as far as the eye could see. It looked just like the pictures of the Napa Valley my grandparents showed me, a place in California once world-renowned for their wines.

Apparently still a booming business, especially with free labor, I thought bitterly.

The road took me for another mile before leading to a tall, wrought-iron gate. It looked similar to Sheol's gate, but a fancier version that could be opened with a push of a button. This one also had what looked like a family crest on it, crafted from a bronze-like metal to stand out against the black wrought-iron.

Wait a minute...

The armed guards tightened their grips on their weapons and walked to the center of the road, but it wasn't them I was leaning forward to see.

That crest looked familiar. I hadn't seen it in years but knew those crossed rifles, the extinct grizzly bear between the stocks, and the letters YB above the gun barrels.

It was *my* family crest.

That was not what I expected to see.

"State your name and business." The guards' leader approached my bike and peeked over his sunglasses to eyeball the patches on my cut. "And your MC and position."

"Gunner Youngblood, Steel Demons MC captain of the guard and arms dealer," I rattled off before nodding at the dude's gun. "Better clean that barrel, sergeant. It's looking pretty fucking filthy."

His jaw clenched, as did his grip on his gun. "What's your business with Governor Youngblood?"

I must have heard him wrong. There was no fucking way.

"Governor?" I repeated. "When did my uncle go from general to governor?"

The guard smirked at my ignorance. "You haven't been around in a while, I see. The governor's become quite ambitious."

"I can see that. A winery in Colorado, huh?"

"You're in the Province of Jerriton, son," the guard said smugly. "Get used to the name, 'cause it's gonna stick around for a *long* time."

"That's what they all say," I returned, still sitting astride my bike as I crossed my arms. "So you gonna let me in to chat with my uncle or what?"

"You haven't stated your business!"

"Family reunion," I said snidely. "The business I have with Uncle Jerry is with him alone. Just tell him his nephew Gunner is at the gate. He'll know what this is about."

The guy's jaw ticked again but he pulled out a radio and mumbled some string of code words into it as he walked back toward the gate. A response came through the scratchy speaker, then he said my name and waited for another reply.

I sighed as I took hold of my grips again. *Jerry, what have you done?* I wondered as I took in the neatly trimmed topiaries, the matching bear statues flanking each side of the gaudy, ornate entryway.

It was ridiculous. Who was he trying to impress with this shit? People just wanted to keep their families together and hold onto what little, meager belongings they still had.

Perhaps a better question was, how many people did

he exploit to achieve this level of wealth? And what gave him the idea to flex like this?

The gate slowly began opening to one side with a metallic cranking sound, while the head guard nodded at me and waved me through.

I took my feet off the ground and drove forward, feeling oddly like going through that gate would seal my fate in a way. There would be no turning back from this.

Uncle Jerry and I shared a bloodline but we weren't family, not like I was with the Demons. I was nothing like him and never would be.

Hopefully he remembered that.

JANDRO

I knocked twice on the door with my free hand, blowing out a deep exhale as I lowered my fist.

Reaper, why are you such a fucking idiot?

Mari cracked open the door a moment later, fully dressed but her face was puffy. She looked like she didn't get a wink of sleep.

"Hi, Jandro." Her voice was raspy and she cleared her throat as she opened the door.

"Morning, Mari." I held out the paper cup and bag. "Brought you coffee and a breakfast burrito. We're riding out in a half hour."

"Okay. Um, thanks." She tucked a strand of hair behind her ear, trying to look poised when all she wanted to do was go back to bed. "Did Reaper send you up?"

I didn't miss the touch of longing in her voice and treaded lightly on what I should say.

"He came down alone about an hour ago, extra

grumpy and looking like he got just as much sleep as you. So I figured something was up."

"Oh." She swallowed. "We, uh—"

"It's okay," I raised a hand. "No need to rehash it while it's fresh. We'll get you home and then go from there."

She forced a tiny smile that made me want to shake Reaper by his dumbass butthurt shoulders.

"Thanks, Jandro. So I'm riding back with you, I guess?"

"If you want to," I told her earnestly. "Nothing says you have to."

"I will, if that's okay. The only other person would be Gunner and he—"

"Will join me in kicking Reaper's ass when he's back," I promised her. "I'm happy to have you ride with me, don't worry about a thing." I couldn't resist a smirk and adding, "I'll behave. Promise."

"I'll believe you *this time*," she replied, smiling like she was forcing herself to be cheerful. "Don't make me regret it."

"Oh, you'll never regret a single minute with me." *Shit, already too much. Pump your brakes, J. She's heartbroken.*

But Mariposa laughed lightly and I saw the hint of a genuine smile. "I'm almost all packed up, so I'll be down in a few minutes. Thanks again for bringing me food."

"Anytime, *Mariposita*. I'll see you down in a few."

Her door clicked softly closed while I muttered curses all the way to the bike garage.

"Where the hell have you been?" Reaper demanded

the moment he saw me. "I need you to sign off on all this cargo strapped to the bikes."

"Yeah well, I'd tell you to sign off my foot up your ass but I don't need your permission for shit."

"...What?"

"I dunno, that was the first thing that popped into my head. But Mariposa is what."

He got within inches of my face right then, scowling hard. "What the fuck did you do?"

"Hm, I'm gonna plead the fifth, Mr. President," I taunted. "'Cause all signs point to, she's no longer yours. Therefore, what *we* do is none of your business."

"I swear to God, Jandro," he leaned in so close, I could've caught his spittle on my face. "If you really swooped in on her like a fucking vulture, I will—"

"Jesus, Reap," I shoved him back out of my face. "Your skin is paper-thin, lately. Of course I didn't do shit. I just brought her coffee and breakfast. Even if I wanted to swoop in, she's too fucking busy crying over you."

His eyes widened, then narrowed again like he wanted to slug me for fucking with him. A resigned sigh escaped him as he leaned against his bike, pinching the bridge of his nose.

"I fucked up, Jandro."

"I'll say."

"I didn't get a chance to tell her anything. Fuck, I don't even know where to begin with that shit."

"What, did you just suggest bringing other dudes into the bedroom?"

"Kind of, yeah."

"Ugh," I groaned, scrubbing my hands down my face. "You fuckers kill me. First I gotta tell Shadow why he should say good morning, now I gotta tell *you* how to not freak out a woman?"

"Fuck off. I've never done this shit before." He pulled out a cigarette, lit it and took a deep drag. "Heather used to beg me to share her. Others did, too."

"But that's like a one-night stand begging for old lady status," I said.

He nodded. "Now the one time I *want* it to happen, she goes off saying I'm just looking for a pass to fuck other women."

"Mari's from Texas," I explained. "She's probably never heard of the matriarchal groups."

"Noelle told her a little about ours but," he shook his head. "Clearly not enough." He sucked on the cigarette once more before tossing the butt away. "Women," he added with a scoff.

"Right," I crossed my arms. "This is all on you, buddy. Your ego got hurt and now let me guess, you're going to be too stubborn to man up and apologize."

"It's not that," he sighed. "I hurt her, J. When she left, I told her to leave the door open for the next girl."

"What?! Dude." I stared at him in disbelief. "You are the king of saying insensitive shit, but *really?*"

"I know. I know." He rubbed his forehead. "I dunno, man, maybe it's best that I just cut her loose."

"You mean cut her out of the club entirely? 'Cause that's the only way she's gonna get over your dumb ass."

"Can't do that," Reaper shook his head. "We need her. Especially if we go to war with Tash."

"Then it's time to put on your big boy pants and send her flowers or some shit, 'cause a girl's heart can only take so much. You have to show that you're sincere."

"How the fuck do you know so much?" he growled.

"Four older sisters, remember?"

"Ah yeah. I forgot."

"What can I say, being surrounded by hot-head Latin women taught me well." I smacked his arm. "It also taught me that women remember literally *everything* you've ever said or done."

"I don't grovel for anyone," Reaper snarled. "Not for a woman, not for a general with a gun at my head. *No one.*"

"If it were anyone else, I'd be right there with you," I said. "But look me in the eye and tell me you're willing to let this one go because of your fucking manly pride."

"Ugh..."

"I know, man." I clapped his shoulder. "But since the hurt is so fresh, you should give her some space first. Do your groveling when we get home."

"But I want to move past this and go back to how it was!"

"It's not about *you*, bro. That's what I'm trying to tell you. *She* needs to let the sting of you hurting her cool down a little. *She* needs to feel confident that you genuinely want this to work. See what I'm saying?"

"Damn it." He kicked at a pebble. "You're right."

"She's riding with me back home. Along with Chela, Perdita, and Letty."

"Who?"

"My chickens," I grinned. "A farm in my back yard don't sound so bad, after all."

"Jesus Christ, Jandro..."

"Hey, don't come knocking at my door for fresh eggs every morning if you're gonna bitch." I gave him a two-fingered salute as I walked off. "See you on the road, *presidente*."

———

"UH, JANDRO?"

"Si, Mariposita?"

"Why is Big G in his underwear?"

I looked up, then quickly ducked my head down to hide my laughter. While the rest of us were decked out in black riding leathers, Big G stood out like a sore thumb wearing nothing but a pair of boxers that showed *way* too much plumber crack. The pasty white boy's skin was already turning pink and had a thin sheen of sweat. Dude was going to be fucking miserable, but he would live.

"Don't worry about him. It's punishment for running his mouth."

"He's going to get a hell of a sunburn."

"Yeah, that's kind of the idea."

Mariposa turned toward my bike, winding her pony-tail up into a bun to shove under her helmet. "Are your chickens going to be okay like that?"

She looked worriedly at the cages I attached with bungie cords to each side of my bike. One held two of my girls, Chela and Perdita, the other held Letty and a rooster I snagged last minute. I decided to call him Foghorn.

"They'll be okay for two days on the road," I assured her. "Once we're home, they'll have my whole back yard to roam."

After talking to Reaper, I decided to grab a male to breed the next generation of chickens. If we were smart about it, Sheol could have its own sustainable, healthy food source. But they had to be treated well and with respect, as much respect as one could give a chicken, anyhow.

My uncle used to work in a USDA-funded slaughter-house. Conditions there were tough enough before the Collapse, but it turned into a straight-up horror movie after regulations and safety standards went right out the window. On top of already being surrounded by blood and death, overworked employees with worthless pay now had access to dangerous weapons and animals to take out their frustrations on.

And people wondered why I was so good with Shadow. I'd been soothing a grown man after his violent nightmares for years already.

"Are you going to build them a coop?" Mari asked with a smile. She stuck a finger through the cage and gently stroked Perdita's feathers.

"I guess I should, huh?" I scratched the back of my neck. "To keep coyotes from getting them."

"Don't ask me to play vet," she laughed. "I don't know anything about bird anatomy."

Together we looked up, finding the familiar sight of Horus perched on the roof just outside the kitchen. I didn't know much about birds either, but hoped the raptor had enough sense to leave my chickens alone.

"You miss Gun?" I caught Mari's wistful expression as she watched Horus take off from the roof.

"Yeah, I do," she admitted. "He took my mind off things and made me laugh last time."

She didn't have to specify. I hated that she got the blunt end of Reaper's silent treatment not once, but twice. She was too good of a woman for his butthurt reactions.

"He'll be back." I tucked a finger under her chin. "And he's going to be happy as hell to see you. In the meantime," I flashed her a grin. "I'll do my best."

"Thanks, Jandro." A soft blush heated her cheeks as her eyelashes fluttered. "You're already helping a lot."

"Anything to see that smile," I dropped my hand reluctantly, "and to see Reaper squirm."

She chuckled as she threw a leg over my bike, securing her helmet in place for the ride. I doubled-checked everything just as Shadow walked up.

"All the weapons and loot from the armory is secure," he reported. "They are heavy on the bikes, though," he added.

"It's tough having one less bike with Gunner gone," I said, rubbing my chin. "We'll keep a moderate pace to not burn fuel too fast. Thanks, man."

"Good morning, Shadow!" Mari piped up.

I knelt next to my front tire to hide my laugh, where I could see Shadow's hand clench into a fist. His eyes slid down to me with a scowl.

"Say it," I mouthed.

"Good morning," he grunted out before turning and high-tailing it back to his bike.

"Wow," I said, rising up to standing. "That's two more words than I've *ever* heard him say to a woman. The next two might be marry me."

"Shut up." Her eyes rolled under her visor. "Why doesn't he talk to women?"

"That's a long, horrendously sad story that isn't mine to tell." My gaze lifted to my big silent friend sitting astride his bike, waiting to go.

"How did you two meet?"

"Through my job before the Collapse." I needed to be on my bike, too, but I didn't want to stop looking at her or talking to her. "I don't mean to be vague but he's uncomfortable with people knowing about his past, so I try to respect that."

"You're a good friend." Her smile was hidden by the helmet but I saw it in the corners of her eyes anyway.

"Thanks, Mari." I threw a leg over my steed, knowing I'd be sitting out here forever if I didn't get moving. "Ready to ride?"

"I'm ready." Her hands slid around my abdomen with more confidence and assuredness than the first time she rode with me.

I almost sighed at her touch on me. And thought for the hundredth time that day how much of an idiot Reaper was.

The roar of his engine suddenly cut through the quiet desert morning. The Steel Demons answered with the growls and revs of our bikes, like a pack of wolves answering their alpha's call. Mari's fingers curled around the edges of my cut.

Hades let out a long, chilling howl before he darted out from the back of the pack. He looked thrilled to run again, jaws open in a wide smile with his tongue lolling out the side.

Reaper followed after him seconds later, his tires kicking up dirt and sand. Damn, I was going to be cleaning the chrome on these steeds until I was stooped over and grey.

We followed after him in our usual procession. Feeling my bike move underneath me was like returning home already. Sure, I had a home base, but the road was where I belonged.

As the Sandia Mountain outpost became a distant speck in my mirrors, I had to remember not to get too comfortable on the journey.

We still had a traitor among us. And it could be any one of these men riding alongside me.

FOURTEEN

MARIPOSA

I forgot how comfortable it was to ride with Jandro.

Something about his tires or the design of his bike made it seem like a relaxing train ride rather than a bumpy desert highway. Even the chickens didn't seem distressed, despite being surrounded by rumbling engines.

Muffled by the padding inside Noelle's helmet, the noise quickly became a soft lull that was almost comforting. Combined with the ease I felt on the back of Jandro's bike, my lack of sleep started catching up with me.

My head wanted to rest on the back of his shoulder a few hours into the ride. My fingers started to slack on their grip around his waist. At one point he grabbed my hand and held it against his chest. I couldn't be sure if he was trying to prevent me from falling off or wanted to touch me for some other reason.

He didn't let go until we stopped for our first break, and it was a slow, gentle release finger by finger.

"Falling asleep on me back there?" he asked when he cut the engine and dismounted.

I pulled my helmet off and shook my hair out. "It feels like a princess carriage," I laughed. "I barely felt the road at all."

"Good. That means my shocks are holding up. I'm gonna have to replace these gaiters, though, the sun and sand are doing a number on 'em."

"English now," I teased. "Or I'll speak only in medical terms."

"Sorry." He shot me an adorably sheepish grin. "I geek out about bikes. And I'd *love* to hear you talk medic to me, baby."

"Well right now," I wiped sweat from my brow and shielded my eyes. "I'd say a *sphenopalatine ganglioneuralgia* is totally worth the risk in this heat."

"Okay, you just made that shit up," he laughed.

"I did not! *Sphenopalatine ganglioneuralgia* is a legitimate medical diagnosis."

"Sounds terrifying. What is it?"

"Brain freeze," I grinned. "From eating ice cream."

"Brain...freeze!" He doubled over his handlebars, laughing so hard he could barely get the words out.

A few heads turned to see what the commotion was. I didn't dare meet any of their eyes, for fear of looking right at Reaper.

"What the fuck! Oh God..." Jandro finally composed himself, even having to wipe tears from his eyes. "Yeah, I sure wouldn't mind a sphino-whatever-the-fuck if I got ice cream out of it."

We all took about a half-hour to stretch our legs

and have bites to eat before Reaper gave the order to ride on. I climbed back on behind Jandro, remembering with sadness that I'd never ridden with Reaper. He'd been all pissed at me on the way to the Sandia outpost, too. We were together, maybe in not a super significant way, but more so than with anyone else. And yet I never rode on the back of his bike.

That time he took me from Old Phoenix didn't count—we'd been tied together by a rope so I wasn't exactly a willing passenger.

An ache filled me at the thought of never holding onto him as the world flew past us. I'd never rest my head on the back of his shoulder like now with Jandro. The vice president's hand caressed mine again, which felt nice but it wasn't Reaper's.

Hell, I didn't know if Reaper would even let me stay in the club after this. With Jandro and Gunner in my corner, I'd hopefully end up okay. But would I really be able to get over seeing Reaper all the time?

The landscape distracted me from my thoughts until dusk approached and we stopped for the night. I offered to set up Jandro's tent and bedroll, partially to be useful but mostly to keep myself busy.

"You're an angel. Thank you." Jandro kissed my temple so quickly, both of us froze and stared at each other as if to say, *did that just happen?*

"Sorry," he mumbled distractedly, jerking his gaze away. "I'm gonna get a fire started."

I set up his sleeping area, all the while still feeling the warmth and pressure of his lips on the side of my head.

Reaper kissed me there a few times, but I came to realize I didn't mind that Jandro did it.

It was nothing like his sneaky neck kiss back at Fight Night. He was playing with me then, deliberately trying to get a rise out of me.

This was different. He seemed like a naturally affectionate person, but wasn't trying to play it up and be all smooth this time. He knew I'd be completely alone with Gunner gone and Reaper ignoring me again. As Reaper's right hand man, I had serious doubts he was being nice to me for his own gain.

I took a moment to stretch out on his sleeping bag, enjoying the quietness and solitude. The Demons' voices were a gentle murmur outside these canvas walls. Just like on his bike, Jandro's tent felt safe and comfortable enough that I could relax completely.

Rolling onto my side, I couldn't resist taking a small whiff. And then a bigger one. Goddamnit, even his sleeping bag smelled good.

"Hey, Mari."

"What!" I shot upright just as Jandro pulled back the flap.

He looked amused at my startled reaction. "Sorry, were you taking a nap?"

"No, no. I was just...resting. What's up?"

"Uh huh," he smirked but chose not to comment. "The fire's going. Come out and make your dinner plate. Then you can rest on my sleeping bag all you want."

"Shut up," I muttered, climbing to my feet and following him out.

The club settled into their familiar evening routine--

drinking, laughing, and swapping stories as the sun set below the horizon. Horus perched on a nearby boulder, preening his feathers next to the fire. It almost felt like Gunner was right there, but had just shifted into his bird friend.

"I miss you, Gun," I whispered.

Horus looked at me with a small head tilt, then made a few chirpy clicks in response.

Throughout the evening, Jandro kept me distracted from looking over at Reaper with stories from his childhood.

"My sister convinced me putting peanut butter in my hair would give me that badass spiky look." He shook his head sadly. "I was the youngest of five and the only boy. It was a nightmare."

"Aww, *pobrecito Alejandro*," I smiled. "That bad to be surrounded by women all the time, huh?"

"Awful. I'm scarred for life," he joked back. "Do you have any siblings?"

"No. Um," I paused and bit my lip nervously. "My parents weren't married when my mom got pregnant with me."

His eyebrows lifted with understanding. "Oh."

"Yeah, they were dating and falling in love anyway, but rushed into marriage to prevent my mom from being ostracized for loose morals." I threw back the rest of my lukewarm beer. "I think that whole experience put her off from having another kid, even though she was safe after getting married."

"They called it seductive witchcraft in Arizona," Jandro sneered. "After raiding the matriarchal communities, officials went on witch hunts for the most ridiculous shit. Women with tattoos, women who were *rumored* to have had children out of wedlock, widows who had remarried. You'd think this was the Salem witch trials after all that bullshit."

"Where are your sisters now?" I asked.

"Last I heard, hiding out in Oregon. I mean, excuse me, the Constitutional Monarchy of Cascadia," he added with an eye roll. "Supposedly one of the safest and most stable places after the Collapse."

"Have you heard from them?"

"I got a letter and a care package from the oldest one about three months ago." He was quiet for a moment, staring into the fire. "The second-youngest got pregnant by a man she's not married to, which worries me a little. But all four of them are super close, and from what I understand, they're all together and supporting her." He chuckled to himself. "And I guess I'm an uncle now."

"Well congratulations, *Tio Jandro.*" I knocked my empty cup against his. "I hope you'll see your sisters again and get to meet your niece or nephew."

"Thanks, *Mariposita.* Me, too."

The darkness of night grew deeper as the fire died down. Men started retiring to their tents, while the first ones on patrol loaded their weapons for their shift. I thought I should try to catch some sleep, too, but felt a stronger pull to keep talking to Jandro.

"So you knew about the matriarchal groups, but weren't a part of them?" I asked.

"Right," he answered. "They sold a bunch of their

handmade goods at a weekly market near us. Our whole household would go, it was our weekly thing. My aunt loved the jewelry that Reaper's mom made, so that's how he and I met."

"Did your aunt know about...?"

"The multiple husband thing? I don't think it was ever *explicitly* said, but it was pretty clear. Reaper's dads would pop in and out of there, hauling supplies or bringing lunch or something. My aunt was Catholic and would pray for Reap's mom every Sunday, but I think it was more asking for protection than anything else. She knew why they formed their communities and was sympathetic to those reasons."

"Your aunt sounds like a kind woman."

"She was," he nodded. "A saint, really. She had to be to run that circus of a household."

He paused to turn to Shadow seated on the other side of him. The big man had been nursing his liquor bottle since we set up camp and seemed to have reached his limit.

"I'll let you tend to your duties, Mr. Vice President," I brushed my pants off as I stood up.

Jandro's head whipped back to face me. "Wait for me in my tent."

I nodded, gathering up our dishes as I headed that way. I kind of figured he wouldn't let me sleep alone, but it was still nice to get that confirmation.

In his tent by a dim flashlight, I unfolded several blankets and laid them out next to his sleeping bag. I wasn't presumptuous enough to assume I'd be sleeping all cuddled up *in* the bag with him. And anyway, I wasn't ready to do that with any other man besides Reaper.

God damn Reaper.

Lying alone in the silent tent with nothing to distract me, the pang of my heartache hit me hard. It was even worse than the night he kicked me out of his room.

I sucked in a shaky breath, willing myself not to cry. Jandro would be in here in a few minutes. He was already being so good to me, he didn't need to deal with this.

Reaper's final words to me seemed to cut physically through my brain matter and heart chambers. Did he really have someone else come to his room that night? Or did he say that just to hurt me? I still couldn't decide which was worse, not even when my thoughts circled like this that night, too.

When the first sob escaped, I slapped a hand over my mouth. *No, he's not worth it. He's across the camp right now, probably jerking himself off to thoughts of someone else. Don't give him another ounce of your power.* But once my body started its physical grieving practice, it was impossible to shut it off.

I curled up onto my side, turning away from the tent's entrance and brought the blanket up high over my shoulder. Hopefully Jandro would think I went straight to sleep and swiftly do the same.

My breath halted in my lungs as I heard him climb inside.

"You asleep, Mari?" he whispered.

I didn't answer, sealing my lips and breath inside myself.

I heard rustling as he took off his boots and settled into his sleeping bag. My heart nearly exploded when I felt his hand on my shoulder.

"You're holding your breath. What's wrong?"

All my air escaped in a shaking, sniffling wheeze. "H-how did you know?"

"Four sisters, remember? I shared a bedroom until I was fourteen. I know all the signs of a girl trying to cry silently." He scooted closer to my back, rubbing a hand up and down my arm. "Talk to me, Mari. I won't talk back if you don't want me to. I can just listen."

"It's nothing," I sniffed, wiping at my nose. "Sorry, don't worry about me."

"Too late for that. And it's not nothing." He scooted closer until I felt his chest brush against my back. Oh shit, he took his shirt off.

I struggled through my shaky breaths as he lay silently behind me, only his hand moving in a soothing motion up and down my arm.

"I'm just," I sniffed, "processing, I guess. Getting over him. I was starting to feel...too much. And I didn't want to get hurt. But I guess that happened anyway."

Jandro said nothing for a few moments, but his hand moved from my arm to make gentle strokes through my hair.

"You want to know a secret about Reaper? Something very few people know?"

"I dunno, Jandro."

"You can't breathe a word of it to anyone, not even him. But I think it's important for you to know."

"Um, okay."

"He's the most sensitive fucker I've ever met."

"What?" My laugh came out like a snort.

"He feels a lot for you, too, and I think that scared *him*. But what happens when he cares about someone is he takes shit *so* personally. Any perceived insult of his character will eat away at his soul. So he'll lash out in response to hurt the person who hurt him."

"Oh my God," I slapped a palm to my forehead. "That's exactly what I made him do. Both times."

"Don't beat yourself up, Mari. We've all taken the brunt of Reaper's temper before. He's been a lot more volatile ever since Daren died."

"I can't believe I never made that connection." A different ache formed in my heart, one of empathy. "He's been hurting the whole time I've known him. How could I miss that?"

"He shoves it down deep," Jandro answered. "Covers it up with that asshole exterior. But the happiest I've seen him in over a year is when he's with you. So you might be healing our president after all, Miss Medic."

I rolled over slowly, the darkness thankfully hiding my puffy face. "Can I be honest with you, Jandro?"

"Always." His hands pulled away from my hair to tuck behind his head.

"I don't know if I can go back to that. Having to watch what I say, dealing with him not talking to me for days if I say the wrong thing. I lov—he means a lot to me, but I can't live like that."

I swallowed the knot in my throat, the weight of what I *almost* said feeling like a brick in my stomach.

"The guy's not perfect, that's for damn sure," Jandro

said. "And you're free to choose your own partner, or *partners*. But if anyone can remove Reap's head from his ass, I'm betting on you."

It was sweet of him to say, but my mind was made up even though my heart disagreed with every pump of blood through me. The heart was stupid, though. That was why it wasn't the brain.

After we got back to Sheol, I wasn't going to be anyone's girl. It didn't matter if they wanted arm candy, casual sex, or something more. I just wanted to be a medic and do what I loved most.

I'd have to move out of Reaper's place most likely, but I'd figure out the logistics of that when the time came. Maybe I could be Gunner or Jandro's roommate. Platonically, of course.

I smiled at the thought of seeing Tessa again. She'd be ready to pop soon and I couldn't wait to deliver and meet her baby. *That* was what I needed to focus on. My work, my calling in life. Not a guy, no matter how good in bed he was.

"Thanks for listening, Jandro." I reached out in the darkness, aiming blindly for a half-hug or maybe a pat on the shoulder. Instead my hand found a flat plane followed by ridges of hard muscle.

"Okay, this is really embarrassing as a medic but what am I touching?"

"You're like a half-inch away from tweaking my nipple. Which you are welcome to do, by the way."

I knew he'd expect me to pull my hand away, and so decided to play his own game and do just the opposite.

"Ow! I said you could *tweak* it, not give me a full-on titty twister!"

"It was too tempting," I laughed, sliding my hands under my head. "I'm learning how you play."

"I'm creating a monster," he chuckled before pulling his sleeping bag over him. "Goodnight, *Mariposita*."

I saw his dark outline lean over to me and I lifted my head without thinking.

The kiss he planted landed at the corner of my mouth.

MARIPOSA

I knew before even fully waking that I ended up in Jandro's sleeping bag. After crying and spilling my guts out to him, I didn't even care.

My head snuggled into his chest, mostly smooth and hairless except for a small strip between his pecs. He was built broader than Reaper, with slightly thicker arms. His smell carried a hint of motor oil alongside clean earth. The same smell I leaned into on the back of his bike, and wrapped around myself in his blankets.

I let out a sigh and nuzzled my face deeper into him, not ready to leave this cocoon of warmth and safety I found. He responded by tightening his arm around me, pulling me flush against his torso.

"You awake?" he mumbled somewhere above my head.

"No."

"Me neither." He sighed contentedly, his chest expanding against my cheek. "You okay like this?"

"Mm hm." My hand drifted along his ribs. "I don't want to move," I confessed.

"Same here, *Mariposita*." He pulled back to look at me and I almost gasped at the sight of his hazel eyes up close. The shifting colors *almost* put Reaper's eyes to shame. "I don't want to make your feelings even more confused," he said.

"I'm not confused," I assured him. "Reaper and I are over."

He cocked an eyebrow, propping his head up with an elbow. "Is that so?"

I nodded. "It's still fresh. I mean, it'll take me a little while to move on. And he has so, *so* many great qualities, but—" I paused, letting it sink in that I was technically in bed with Reaper's best friend while gabbing about him.

"But he's Reaper and he's kind of exhausting," I finished.

Jandro looked at me curiously. "He never told you how relationships work with him, right?"

"All he said was he didn't do traditional relationships. I just figured that meant he liked to play the field." I ran a hand through my hair. "I thought I was okay with that but I guess not."

"I see," Jandro mused as if I had somehow answered wrong. "Well," he straightened his arm so his head flopped back down, "as much as I'd like to stay here all day, we gotta get moving."

"Ugh." I buried my face in his chest again, bracing my arm against his back to hold him in place.

He just chuckled as he dropped a kiss to the top of

my head. "I'll bring you coffee." His hands stroked my hair and back as he made his offer.

"Fine," I grumbled, reluctantly letting go.

Jandro rolled away from me lazily, pulling on his jeans and boots but didn't bother with a shirt.

I watched him leave the tent, basking in the warmth of the spot he just left. He didn't make this weird, which he easily could have. I cried and lamented my heartache over his best friend all while basically spooning with him. Then I spent the night in his arms and in the morning, we talked about me and his best friend some more.

He made it all seem so...*normal*. Just being in his presence felt soothing and like a safe place to get things off my chest. It made me wonder how many people came to him with their problems. How many people who had no one, and like me, he took them under his proverbial wing.

I was still fully dressed except for my boots, so I pulled those on and pushed open the tent flap to see who was up.

Jandro was talking to Shadow, who was in a short-sleeved T-shirt for the first time that I saw. The texture on his forearms made me do a double-take.

Rows of scars crisscrossing and overlapping ran from his wrist and disappeared under his sleeve. They were pale and thin, clearly several years old, and looked like self-harm scars. Which wasn't that unusual but there were *so many*.

"*Un cafe para la Mariposita.*" Jandro pulled my attention away as he approached with two cups of coffee.

"Gracias." I accepted the steaming tin mug from him and cupped my palms around it. By the time my attention returned to Shadow, he pulled on his signature black long-sleeved shirt and was shrugging on his cut.

"Looks like Foghorn and the girls made it through the night." Jandro bent over the cages still affixed to his bike. All four birds appeared calm, either sitting or preening themselves. "Don't worry, you guys will be out before the end of the day."

"When do you expect to reach Sheol?" I asked.

"Before nightfall," he answered. "In plenty of time for a homecoming barbecue but I think everyone's gonna want to crash at home tonight. We'll throw a party tomorrow night." His eyes brightened as he looked at me. "Feeling homesick?"

"A little, yeah," I admitted.

His eyebrows lifted in surprise. "For Texas or Sheol?"

"Sheol," I clarified. "Texas changed so much in the last few years and I've been away for so long," I shook my head. "It's not my home anymore."

"Well, I'll be damned," he smirked. "Bet you never thought you'd consider a biker club home, huh?"

"I know," I laughed. "I miss Noelle and Tessa. I'm *dying* for pregnancy updates! I miss the little medic's office." My fingers drummed on my cup with a thought that popped into my head. "Do you know if the kids in the club are vaccinated?"

"They're not. A lot of the adults aren't either." Jandro sipped from his cup. "Even flu shots haven't been affordable for normal people in at least ten years."

"I'd like to start vaccinating everyone in the club

then, if that's okay," I said. "I have a small stockpile of the essentials, but maybe Gunner can get me more. With the lack of medical care and rise of preventable diseases, I'd like to give the kids a chance at a higher quality of life."

"That's fine with me. I'll bring it up at the next church meeting." He grinned at me. "You are in *much* better spirits today, *Mariposita*."

"I feel better," I admitted. "And I owe a lot of it to you." My eyes fell to my coffee, a rush of shyness taking over. "Thanks for being there, Jandro. I needed someone just to lean on and listen, and there you were."

"Don't mention it," he said softly. "I'm always here for the ones that matter to me." A warm beat of silence passed between us before I pressed my mug back into his hand. "Thanks for the coffee. I'll get everything packed up. You do what you need to get this show on the road."

"Mmkay. Let me know if you need any help." He leaned over and kissed the edge of my cheekbone before walking off.

I watched him for a few paces, reaching up to touch where his lips made contact with my skin for a fraction of a second. He did it so casually, like it was the most normal thing to do.

And maybe it was. Cheek kisses were common displays of affection between platonic friends and even family members in Latin cultures. I wasn't sure when that barrier broke or whether it *was* completely platonic. But as I watched his broad shoulders swagger away, I realized it didn't matter. Kisses, coffee, a listening ear, or a gentle tease—all gestures that were Jandro's way of showing he cared.

I broke down his tent, watching as he paused to talk with Shadow, giving the big man a slap on the shoulder before moving on. Something else occurred to me then. Jandro wasn't just a caring guy, but the club's caretaker.

While Reaper barked orders and grumbled like a hungover bear, Jandro went around like the club dad and made sure everything got done. Shadow always stayed closest to him, like a son would hover near his father. The dynamic was so clear to me now, I couldn't believe I didn't notice earlier.

Reaper ignored me all morning, as expected. It still stung but not as badly as before. I'd probably have another good cry or two before it stopped hurting, but at least I wasn't completely alone anymore.

The whole club packed up and was on the road again within an hour. I leaned unabashedly against Jandro on his bike this time, even running my hands across his chest and abs. We played a game where I tried to tweak his nipple before he stopped me. He'd get me back by reaching behind to poke or tickle me.

On the last leg of the ride, the final stretch before reaching home, we stopped with the games. Everyone was exhausted and dying to sleep in their own beds. Jandro occasionally ran his hand down the side of my leg. When I massaged his chest, he brought my fingers to his lips and kissed them. After debating it for the last hundred miles, I placed a kiss on the back of his neck. His heart sped up under my hand.

I didn't know if this would lead anywhere but in the

meantime, it was a fun distraction. Whatever the outcome, I knew Jandro wouldn't lash out at me like Reaper had.

The sky exploded into a brilliant sunset display—pinks, purples and oranges like it was on fire. I was enthralled by the view when Jandro squeezed my thigh to get my attention.

"Home sweet home!" he yelled over the engines, pointing straight ahead on the horizon.

I squinted and could just barely make out the tall, wrought-iron gate surrounding the community of Sheol. A tiny speck hovering in the distance, the black flag with the Steel Demons emblem flapped as if beckoning us home.

"SKREEEEEK! SKREEK! SKREEK!"

"Whoa, Horus!" I almost pulled Jandro and I off balance with how closely Gunner's falcon screeched in my ear.

He flew right alongside us, so close I could reach out and stroke his wing. And the screeching never stopped. He almost sounded panicked.

"What is it?" I asked the bird. Dread pooled in my stomach. Something wasn't right.

Horus cut away, angling like a fighter jet as he shot upward in a straight line, until he became a tiny dark speck in the sky.

"Jandro, I think something's—"

"Whoa, Hades!"

He braked as he turned sharply, drifting a few feet to miss Reaper's dog who ran straight in front of us. Hades sprinted to our left, while Horus had taken off to the right. What the fuck were the animals doing? The whole club slowed to a stop in the middle of the empty road.

"Reaper, what's gotten into Hades?" someone asked.

"He senses danger, but I have no clue." Reaper squinted in the direction his furry beast ran off to. "Someone get me a pair of binoculars."

I looked in the opposite direction and found the dark dot in the sky that was Horus. He hovered at a high altitude, almost directly above us from our perspective.

Then he divebombed.

The adorable little bird of prey turned into a missile, hurtling toward the earth almost too fast for my eyes to follow. I almost screamed. He was going to splat against the ground!

But in the last few seconds, his wings stretched out and his claws extended. Gunner's bird was hunting. And when he hit his target, I could see his prey was much bigger than him.

There were several of them and they were coming straight for us. I could barely make out shapes in the distance but they were definitely person-sized.

A low, constant rumble made me turn my head to the left. Hades' prey was much closer and approaching fast. Men on motorcycles formed one dark line on the horizon.

"J-Jandro," I whispered, clutching his shoulders.

"Steel Demons, draw your weapons!" Reaper bellowed, already wielding a handgun. "We're getting ambushed!"

SIXTEEN

GUNNER

The guard detail beyond the gate led me down a long, winding driveway—freshly paved as the private road had been. I could still smell the asphalt.

In the distance, a massive house loomed up ahead. I couldn't even really call it a house, it looked like a fucking castle. We had pretty sweet digs back at Sheol, but this place even made Reaper's mansion look like a shack. It sprawled out to the sides and had tall spires that seemed to pierce the clouds.

Uncle Jerry, what have you done...

Some dude in a suit waited for me at the wide, arching front door. I drove around a huge ornate water fountain and pulled up to the bottom of the shallow steps where he stood.

"Mr. Youngblood," he said in a crisp accent. "Your uncle is pleasantly surprised at your visit. I'm his butler. You may call me Chandler."

A butler? What fucking year was it again?

"Call me Gunner." I dropped my feet to the ground

but left my bike idling. "Wouldn't want you getting my uncle and I mixed up now."

He aimed a tense, patronizing smile at me. "I wouldn't dream of it. You may park your vehicle in the garage if you continue on this road. Security will bring you inside to a sitting room, where you may wait until Governor Youngblood is ready to receive you."

"Thanks," I couldn't help but sneer the word out, "Chandler."

I was ready to eat my words when the garage door pulled up. "Holy shit," I breathed.

A car enthusiast's wet dream laid out before me. The cherry red Corvette caught my eye first—the thing had to be over a hundred years old and was still in pristine condition—but I also recognized BMWs, Mercedes, and even a Mach 1 Mustang that had to be from 1969. That thing wasn't just a car, but an *artifact*.

Whether in a luxury or sporty mood, Uncle Jerry had fine tastes.

I parked next to a BMW 8 series and went with the guard who kept mugging me from across the garage. He told me to wait in a room filled with stuffy furniture that was probably worth more than my bike and all the weapons I had on me combined. I was ready to put up a stink if any of these guards demanded I come in unarmed. But no one did, which meant security sucked at their job or Uncle Jerry had enough of his own firepower for it to not matter.

Chandler came to fetch me after about fifteen minutes, leading me through a long hallway with a tall, domed ceiling. Aside from him, the guards, and what looked like cleaning staff, not many other people seemed to be milling about the mansion. I couldn't decide if that was a good or bad thing.

Chandler knocked three times on a set of ornately-carved double doors—again with the Youngblood family crest. My insides churned at the sight of it. I purposely distanced myself from my blood relatives only to find myself right back in their shenanigans again.

The butler pulled the doors open right after knocking, revealing a comfortable study inside. It reminded me a little of Reaper's study at his house, only much bigger. Dark wooden accents, soft leather chairs, and warm yellow lamplight.

But here, a young blonde woman was straightening her clothes as she stood up from behind the desk in the center of the room. Pink lipstick was smeared on her chin. She was beautiful, but her green eyes looked cold and dead.

"Gunner!" my uncle cried out jovially, raising his arms out as if awaiting a hug. "It's been so long!"

He was sweating a little under his expensive smoking jacket and he panted slightly.

"Howdy, uncle," I returned flatly. "Didn't mean to interrupt anything."

"Not at all, Katya was just leaving." His eyes slid over to the blonde who took her cue to leave. "Can I get you anything?" His attention zapped back to me. "A drink? A cigar?"

"Sure, I'll take one of each."

"Excellent. Chandler!" He snapped his fingers. "Bring us a couple of Cubans and that bourbon I save for special visitors." He chuckled to himself. "You think we can still call it bourbon if Kentucky's not on the map anymore?"

"Why change a good thing, right?" I lowered myself into one of the chairs across from his desk. "So, seems you've done well for yourself, *governor*." I flexed my hands up to indicate the whole room. "Province of Jerriton, huh?"

"Oh, you know I've always been ambitious, Gunner," he grinned at me from across the desk. "All the men in our family are."

"Yeah, about that." I paused to accept the cigar from the silver tray held out by Chandler. "We're not family." I struck the match and lit the end, puffing on the dried, burning tobacco worth a small fortune. Once I got it going, I took the glass of bourbon on the silver tray. "I'm here because my *real* family did you a solid when they could have just as easily let you get killed. They didn't, so you owe a large part of your success to SDMC, *governor*." I exhaled slowly. "And I'm here to cash in on what you owe us."

"Still running around with that gang, are you?" my uncle remarked, lighting his own cigar. "You're almost thirty now, Gun. Don't you think it's time you settled down, started thinking about the future?"

"The future is fucked," I retorted. "It'll take decades to recover from the Collapse, if we ever do. Neither one of us will see a return to order in our lifetimes, so who gives a fuck? I ride hard and live like I'll die tomorrow because that's exactly what might happen. And you know what?" I turned sideways in his cushy chair, throwing my legs up over the armrest. "I've never been happier. Life is fucking good when you live it one day at a time."

"That's so typical of a young buck like you to say." Uncle Jerry leaned back, propping his feet up on his desk. "But planning for the future doesn't mean you have to sacrifice a fun life in the present." He spread his arms wide. "As you observed, I've done well for myself in a short amount of time."

"Yeah, how'd you manage that?" I didn't bother to hide the disdain creeping into my voice. "General to governor isn't exactly a straight climb up the corporate ladder."

"Are you lecturing *me* about survival tactics in a post-Collapse world, mister outlaw biker?" he chuckled patronizingly. "I haven't done anything you wouldn't approve of for yourself or one of your outlaw brothers."

"Right. Here's the difference between you and me, Uncle Jerry." I swung my feet back down to the floor, looking at him straight on. "A Steel Demon doesn't play politics. You couldn't pay me enough to stab one of my brothers in the back, no matter what the personal gain might be. And while we're the furthest thing from saints, we don't use people like machinery or sex toys. Whether we're buying weapons or women for the night, we pay fairly. All this shit," I gestured around the room, "and that dead-eyed, broken girl sucking your dick under your desk? I don't want any part of it. Hell, I'd drop the Youngblood name if I could."

He didn't say anything for a few moments that seemed to stretch on, but just watched me with a guarded expression as the cigar smoke swirled around him. The guy went from popular actor to decorated general because of his charm and charisma, but he was also manipulative and crafty as hell. I didn't trust him as far as I could blow smoke.

Under the former governor of the Colorado territory, Jerry kept the borders fairly consistent as when it was a US state and maintained independence from all the surrounding power grabs post-Collapse. Because of this, the state government held on much longer than most other former states. Colorado was known as a utopia of order, safety, and stability in the chaos that followed the Collapse. People flocked here by the thousands over the last five years. I was with Uncle Jerry in the broadcasting room when he announced over the radio that anyone was welcome in Colorado. The citizens, military, and governor at the time all trusted him.

Then he took that trust and brutally abused it.

Not long after thousands of new citizens got settled in, he recruited women for a "job fair." It turned out that job was servicing his soldiers and not being allowed to leave.

Frantic spouses, siblings, children, and parents all petitioned General Youngblood to find their missing loved ones, not knowing they were being held in cells right beneath their feet.

Until one woman escaped.

The public rioted when they found out what my uncle had done. His personal guard and the small military units with him were quickly overwhelmed. The Steel Demons were just passing through at the time of the riots and I had stopped by for a visit, as we were more cordial back then.

He threw himself down at my feet, begging for protection with tears in his eyes, just until the rest of the army came down from the capital. I told him he deserved a pitchfork up his ass for what he did to those women. I never should have listened to his hysterical whimpering about family and being there for each other. I should have kept walking. Everything would have played so differently if I had.

But had I done so, I wouldn't have him now in my back pocket for when General Tash fucked us. And as much as I hated to admit it, a governor would be a hell of a lot more useful than just another general.

"Fair enough, Gunner," my uncle finally said light-heartedly, although I knew for a fact he wouldn't let this go so easily. "What can I do for you and your adopted biker family?"

"We had a falling out with our biggest trade partner and need a replacement," I cut right to the chase. "We have a surplus of weapons right now, and I have good working relationships with firearm suppliers and manu-facturers. Assuming you want to grow and expand the influence of your new province, you'll want to keep your position protected."

"What if I already have weapons deals?" he said smugly.

"That's fine, keep them. But as your province grows, you'll need more. Consider it an investment for the future," I used his own words right back at him.

"And in exchange, you want…?"

"Food, toiletries, clothing, motor oil and fuel, medical supplies, tools for home and vehicle maintenance," I counted on my fingers as I rattled off the basic necessities. "And building materials such as lumber and sheet metal on an as-needed basis."

"For how many people?"

"Around thirty. Mostly men, but some women and kids. A few pets."

"What are you running, a commune out there?" Jerry scoffed.

"Basically," I answered. "We have a permanent home with a thriving community. Taking care of our people is a priority."

"I see." His response was carefully measured. "This sounds like an exchange to me. A fair one, I might add, which still leaves me in your debt. How do you intend to cash in on your favor?"

"I'm so glad you asked." I took a hearty sip of bourbon. "Our former trade partner is a general who double-crossed us. He led us into a trap and tried to have us executed. We escaped with no casualties, but retribution must be paid for what he did."

My uncle swallowed. For the first time, he seemed nervous.

"Retribution as in?"

"Death. A nice, slow public execution. It's been a long time since my president's done one of those and he's probably itching for it. But we need manpower. This general has his own army, plus agreements with other MCs."

Jerry's face paled a little. "What's the general's name?"

"Renold Tash. He's holding power just south of here in the old New Mexico territory, which he's going to rename New Ireland, apparently. The territory has no governor as of yet. He's expected to take the seat himself or appoint someone."

"Gunner," Jerry shook his head with a grave expression. "I can't help you. Tash and I are in the middle of a ceasefire."

"So?" I retorted. "Break it."

"I can't."

"What, you don't like going back on your word when the other guys are pointing guns at you?" I mocked.

"Gunner, I have to be smart about this—"

"Oh, I understand. You only lie to those who are completely defenseless, got it."

"Gunner!" He coughed out my name with a thick cloud of cigar smoke. "If I play my cards right, there's a chance he'll sell me part of the New Mexico territory. My province could expand by twenty percent in one move and with no casualties. Think of all the goods I can trade with you then!"

I gave him a long hard look of bewilderment.

"Did you not hear a word I said? Everything was going fine, then he tried to have us executed! You don't think he'll do the same to you?"

"You've never been a general, so let me explain something to you, son," Jerry leaned across his desk. "We like hiring MCs because our hands stay clean while you all do the dirty work. And y'all are a dime a dozen, I'm afraid. When we no longer need your services, you're disposable."

"Not the Steel Demons," I hissed. "No other MC can touch us. Treat us like we're disposable and we'll return the gesture right back."

"Even so," Jerry tented his fingers. "General Tash and I have a mutual respect for each other. We both served our country, back when this place still *was* a country. And now we've carved out our own little empires. I'll always have a soft spot for you because you're my brother's kid, but I can't say I have the same respect for those thugs you ride with."

I threw my head back and laughed. Once I started, I just couldn't stop. My stomach ached but the laughter kept coming. I sucked in enough of a breath to say, "Should've thought of that before you begged us to protect you. Oh God…"

When my laughter finally ceased, I drained the rest of the bourbon, stood up, and ashed my cigar right on Jerry's desk.

"What are you doing?!" he demanded, gasping as the charred, circular mark permanently embedded into the expensive wood.

"Remember this, Uncle." I pointed at him with the cigar. "You and Tash may not ride, and you may not wear patches, but you're bigger thugs than we'll ever be."

I tossed the rest of the cigar carelessly and let it roll across his desk, but didn't wait to see where it ended up. I was already out the door.

MARIPOSA

"Weapons out!"

"Tighten up, come in close!"

"Shoot their tires!"

Pure chaos surrounded me. The Steel Demons yelled back and forth, repositioned their bikes, ran to others' bikes to grab guns and ammo. And I just sat frozen and watched.

Reaper brought two fingers to his mouth and blew a long whistle.

"We're outnumbered, so do not group up like sitting ducks, Demons," he roared. "Ride your fucking bikes like you just came out of Hell! Make 'em chase you! No one fucks with us and our home!" He raised a pistol in the air, which I realized was a flare gun. "Let's spill some blood tonight!"

His men answered him with a roar of engines and clouds of dust. They peeled off the road one by one, heading off in different directions, but all going toward the enemy about to close in on us.

Reaper fired the flare into the sky before tossing the gun and brandishing one of the biggest handheld assault rifles I'd ever seen.

"Mari, come here." Jandro barked out the Reaper-esque command. "Sit in front and face me."

Only when I tried to move did I realize I was shaking like a leaf, so he grabbed and physically moved me to sit in front of him. I sat between his arms and the handlebars, straddling his thighs and looking directly at his rare, stern expression.

"Jandro, I'm scared," I confessed, my teeth chattering like I was freezing.

"I know, baby. Just do what I say and you'll be fine, I promise. Take this." He shoved a pistol in my hand.

"I don't know how to use it!"

"Point it at a bad guy and pull the trigger." In his other hand, he cocked an assault rifle of his own. "Tell me when you're out of ammo. And whatever you do, do not put your hands on my back. I'm shielding you, do you understand?"

"But that leaves you exposed!"

"Exactly. I'm going to draw them away from the gate so the others can pick them off." He cupped my face and kissed me too quickly for either of us to enjoy it. "We're going to make it through this, trust me."

"Jandro," my hands shook so hard, I was in serious danger of dropping my gun, "I can't—"

"You *can*. Hold on, we've gotta move."

Everyone else was gone. Only we were left between the two lines of hostile bikers converging in on us.

Jandro weaved his bike in a wide, lazy figure-eight pattern.

"Keep your arms tucked in and hold tight onto my shirt," he instructed. "I'm gonna zig-zag like hell. Only point your gun when you have a clear shot. Got it?"

I nodded, despite feeling nowhere near like I had it.

"Jandro..."

"I know, I know. Trust me."

The roars of at least twenty bikes filled my ears. I could make out their faces now—hard, angry, and ready to kill.

I only hoped the Steel Demons were more ready.

Jandro looped the bike around back the way we came and accelerated hard. Our enemies picked up speed to give chase.

"Tuck in! Stay close!" Jandro yelled.

I curled into him just as his rifle hand pulled away to point behind him. Seconds later came the *rat-tat-tat-tat-tat* of his rapid firing.

The air grew thick with dust kicked up from all the bikes. My eyes burned and I thought I might fall at any moment with Jandro weaving back and forth at such high speed.

He kept looking back to shoot behind us while I clung to him with my tiny silver weapon in my hand.

"Watch out!" I screamed.

One of the riders broke off from his pack and was coming straight for us. We were going to collide head-on, but Jandro was dealing with the dozen or so chasers on our tail.

I shakily aimed my gun and waited. The biker

smiled cruelly and let go of his handlebars to aim his shotgun with both hands.

Somehow, I fired first.

"Fuck!" He clutched at his side. I barely grazed him, but it was enough to surprise him and throw his balance to send him tumbling off of his bike. Jandro maneuvered us out of the way at the last second.

"Nice, Mari!" he praised.

Unseating one of their riders seemed to piss off our chasers even more. They returned Jandro's fire even more rapidly. Bullets whizzed by us and made *plink* sounds as they hit the frame of his bike.

"Ah!" Jandro's torso jolted forward, his face a grimace of pain and his knuckles white on the grips.

I touched his shoulder, my palm coming away red and sticky. "You're hit!" I cried.

"Keep your hands in front!" he bellowed.

"You're bleeding a lot!"

"Up ahead, WATCH OUT!"

I looked behind me, my arm already extended with the pistol. This time I hit the rider coming at us right in the torso. He slumped over his bike, which careened into a cluster of sharp boulders. Bodies and abandoned bikes already began piling up.

Bodies, fuck!

I tried to scan the faces of men strewn out among the landscape, but we were moving too fast. Some Demons must have gotten hurt, though. We were far too outnumbered and I had to save who I could. Jandro's bullet wound bloodied half of his shirt already but at least he was still riding.

"Jandro, I have to treat the wounded!"

"You're not getting off this bike," he growled, sweat beading on his forehead. "They'll steal you from us. You're too valuable."

"But your men could be dying!" *Oh God, Reaper!*

I hadn't seen him since he fired off that flare, which I could only assume was a distress signal to his men still inside Sheol. But with all the dust, the bikes, the noise and the chaos, I couldn't make out who was friend or foe.

"Reaper!" I yelled to Jandro. "We've got to find Reaper!"

If I was scared before, I was in a full-blown panicked meltdown now. The Steel Demons president *had* to be alive. He didn't even seem worried about going to battle —if anything, he seemed excited despite the odds not looking good. But if Jandro was taking shots, surely the others were, too.

"I know babe, but we gotta live through this first —gah!"

Another bullet grazed his arm, creating a surface wound that quickly pooled blood on his skin. It was his shooting arm, too, which I knew was becoming fatigued.

Still he raised it again, spraying gunfire behind us to mow down the three closest riders on our tails.

"Jandro, I need to slow your bleeding," I pleaded. "And we need to find Reaper, and anyone else who's hurt."

His gaze was sharp, but his breathing was ragged and he could barely hold himself up. Adrenaline pushed him to keep going but he was losing blood quickly. Just when it looked like he'd give in to my request, something caught his eye up ahead of us.

"Hold onto me. We're gonna roll."

"My pack!" I cried just before he pulled me against his torso and lurched us to one side.

For the briefest moment, I felt nothing but air. Then the hard ground knocked the wind out of me and the world spun as we went rolling. My vision kept spinning even as we came to a stop and Jandro pulled us behind a couple of crashed bikes for cover.

"What...what?" was all I could say.

"They dug potholes," he panted, wincing at the pain. "To catch our front tires and send us flipping over our handlebars." He forced a grin and held up his rifle, which had the strap of my medic pack barely hanging onto the end of the barrel. "Got you this, though."

"You probably just saved your own life then." I grabbed it from him and quickly pulled out my gauze and tape. "I'll have to look at it later but you won't bleed out now."

"Shit, shit, hide!"

Jandro shoved me against the makeshift wall of twisted metal, but it was too late. A rider pulled up, coming to a stop in front of us.

"What's this? A Steel Demon hiding like a little bitch?" the rider taunted, pointing his weapon at us. "And with a woman," he added, his voice going higher with interest.

"Take me as a hostage if you want but leave her alone." Jandro raised his arms.

I stared at him. "Jandro, no!"

"Fucking dumbass. Unless you're hiding a pussy, I have no reason to take you over her. Besides," he grinned evilly. "We have strict orders to eliminate your whole club, and take no prisoners. A woman, however—"

"I'm the vice president," Jandro pointed to his patch. "I'm a valuable bargaining chip. She's just a used-up piece of ass. You won't get anything out of her."

"All that's tellin' me is I should shoot you both."

He cocked his gun and raised it to aim. Jandro jumped in front of me.

"Wait, wait!" he protested.

"No..." I grabbed his shoulders and shut my eyes with my forehead against his back.

The shot rang out and his body jerked.

"No!" I cried, clutching him tighter.

But he was still standing on his own.

"Shadow, you motherfucker!" he yelled.

I peeked open one eye and peered over his shoulder. The biker's limp, lifeless body hung over his handlebars. Shadow approached from the left side and grabbed the man's body to haul it off the bike. When the man's head fell back, a dark, bloody hole decorated his forehead.

"Where the fuck is our backup?" Jandro growled before turning around and squeezing me tightly against him. "It's okay."

I couldn't reply. I was shaking again. How could he be so calm? He almost *died*.

"I don't know," Shadow answered his question distractedly while looting through the dead biker's pockets.

"Check his cut," Jandro instructed while rubbing my back. "Who are these shit heads?"

Shadow kicked the body over onto its back, then leaned over to inspect the patch.

"Razor Wire," he reported.

"Of course. In the pocket of General Tash, I'm assuming," Jandro grumbled. "How many of them are left? And how many of us?"

"I've taken down five, including this one," Shadow answered. "As for us, I don't know. It's impossible to see through this dust."

"Reaper!" I remembered now that my own life was safe. "You haven't seen him anywhere?"

Shadow's dark eye passed over me briefly, the pale one still hidden under his hair. "No," he answered.

"We've taken about six or seven down," Jandro said. "Mari shot two herself."

Shadow did not look impressed. "So that's twelve, out of roughly twenty-five total that I counted. To our eight."

"Ten," Jandro corrected. "You know Hades and Horus had to have gotten a couple of kills. They're in the fray just like we are."

"I haven't seen them either."

"Uh, guys?"

"Shit," Jandro cursed at the line of bikers, at least eight of them, coming straight for us on the other side of our cover. "Shadow, give me a full clip."

The large man opened his cut to reach into an inside pocket. It was hard to tell with him wearing all black, but his shirt was wet and sticky with blood.

"Shadow, did you get hit, too?"

He glanced up, surprise on his face before his eyes flicked over to Jandro.

"You definitely got shot, bro," Jandro confirmed.

"Must just be a graze," Shadow mumbled as he reloaded his weapon. "I didn't feel an entry point."

"Let me clean that up real quick," I reached into my pack.

"No," Shadow barked. "We've got incoming. There's no time."

"I'll be fast. It'll just slow your bleeding—"

"I said no!" he snarled at me.

My hands froze in shock. Not because he said no, but the *way* he said it. The way he looked at me when he said it. He glared at me like an injured animal backed into a corner, a mixture of intense fear and defensiveness.

"He'll be okay, Mari," Jandro said with a hand on my shoulder. "Duck behind the bikes and let us handle these fuckers first."

He physically shoved my head down so that I sat on the ground, then he and Shadow braced their assault rifles on top of the crashed bikes which served as our cover.

"Back away a bit, Mari. They're gonna return fire."

They started shooting right as I got moving, covering my head the moment I heard the *plink-plink-plink* of returned fire ricocheting off of metal.

"Just like shooting wooden ducks at the state fair!" Jandro laughed.

"They're still coming," Shadow said.

"Yeah, fuck! They're going around! Get 'em!" Jandro and Shadow slowly turned their rifles as the riders came around in a wide circle. Soon they'd be behind our cover and free to fill our bodies with bullet holes.

The engines grew louder, sounding slightly differently this time and...coming from a different direction?

I looked toward Sheol where the dust started to clear. It was only a few hundred yards away, and yet seemed impossibly far. Visibility was improving though and from inside the gate, I saw what looked like long ramps placed against the wrought-iron supports. And the strange engine sound seemed like it was coming from *inside* the Steel Demons compound.

"Jandro," my voice shook. "Do you hear that?"

"My ears are ringing, babe. I can't hear shit."

Shadow, however, cocked his head toward the direction of the sound.

"I think our backup's finally here."

The sound grew louder. I saw movement inside the gate and my mouth fell open at a sight I never expected to see.

Motorcycles flying through the air.

EIGHTEEN

MARIPOSA

One after another, riders on dirt bikes drove up the ramps and flew into the air to join us in battle. Their engines made higher-pitched grinding sounds, as opposed to the deep rumbles of the road bikes. The dirt bikes were also much smaller and lightweight. They hit the ground with a small bounce like a spring and rode on.

Some of the new riders carried guns, others wielded swords or machetes, but all were armed and ready Steel Demons.

"Fucking finally!" Jandro yelled.

Assuming all of our people were still alive, our numbers were now more evenly matched.

Reaper. I still had to find him. Or at least *see* him to know he was okay.

I hovered behind Jandro as he and Shadow kept shooting over our protective wall of crashed bikes. The returned fire gradually slowed down to nothing and then they stopped.

"Is it over?" I whispered.

"Don't know yet," Jandro muttered. "God, I wish we had Gunner's eyes right now."

One of the dirt bike riders emerged from a cloud of dust, a rifle slung across their back as they stopped in front of us.

"You got my boots and jacket all dirty, bitch!" a feminine voice snarled from inside the helmet.

"What?"

The dark visor flipped up to reveal familiar green eyes, the corners crinkled up from her cheeky grin.

"Noelle!" I screeched, on the verge of tears. "I didn't know you, uh—"

"Could ride and shoot? I'm the president's sister, dummy. Come here."

She lowered her kickstand and hopped off, arms open for my bone-crushing hug as I ran up to her.

"I'm so fucking happy to see you," I whispered against the side of her helmet.

"Same here, Mari. You look good dolled up in my shit." She pulled back from my hug, still smiling. "Speaking of my punk ass brother, where is he?"

"I don't know." The worry creeped back into my voice, taking over my relief. "These guys haven't seen him either."

"Is it clear out there, Noelle?" Jandro addressed her for the first time.

"No Razor Wire on wheels left. Some might be hiding or trapped under fallen bikes. I say we look for our people but proceed with caution."

"I thought *I* was VP?" Jandro teased, grinning at her.

"Tell 'em it was your idea. Y'all have been doing that for hundreds of years already," she joked back. "Mari, want to ride with me?"

"No, she stays with us. She's—"

"I can protect her, Jandro," Noelle rolled her eyes. "You guys got wheels?"

"Yeah, somewhere around here."

"Find 'em then meet us back inside the gate." Noelle threw a leg over her bike and looked at me. "I'm guessing you're going to have a few patients once we get everyone in."

I nodded, climbing on behind her and holding onto her waist. "If anyone has stretchers or long carts we can pull people in, we might need them for any leg wounds or head injuries."

"Got it." She kicked off the ground and off we went. "A couple guys have pickup trucks, we can put people in the truck beds. Anything else we should prepare for?"

"I'll just need extra hands," I said. "To apply pressure to wounds, to hand me tools if I need to do surgery. I won't know for sure until I see what injuries people have."

"You've got me, girl," Noelle patted my hand on her stomach. "I'll rally some other help, too. Don't you worry."

"Thank you," I sighed. "God, it's so good to see you."

"You mean you weren't in heaven surrounded by dick all day?" she laughed.

"That's not exactly what I would call it."

We passed by two other dirt bike riders and Noelle yelled at them to get pickup trucks.

The dust was now settling but night was falling. Noelle turned her headlight on as we maneuvered through bodies and debris.

"There's Big G!" I pointed and Noelle pulled straight up to him.

He got shot in the calf and would definitely need to be carried home, but thankfully he managed to get some clothes on at some point. I wrapped gauze around his wound, gave him a pill for pain and told him to sit tight. The trucks would be coming soon and he just had to wave them down.

"Poor Tessa," Noelle muttered as we drove away. "She's about to deal with four children instead of three."

"What do you mean?" I asked.

"Big G turns into a big toddler when he gets a cold. With a gunshot wound? Poor Tess is gonna be run ragged taking care of his ass."

"We'll help her," I affirmed with a squeeze around Noelle's waist. "I've been dying to see her and listen to her belly again."

"Oh, she'll be thrilled to see you."

We found a couple more Demons with fairly serious but not life-threatening injuries. I patched them up as well as I could, told them help was on the way, and moved on. But still no signs of Reaper.

When Noelle drove slowly past a big pile-up of motorcycles, I thought I saw movement inside.

"Wait!" I told her. "I think someone's trapped."

She parked her bike and cocked her gun, grabbing my arm as I hopped off. "Stay behind me. It could be one of the other guys."

I nodded, letting her approach the pile of metal with her gun drawn.

"Anyone in there?" she called.

"Help! I'm stuck!" a voice called out.

Noelle looked over her shoulder at me. "Who's that? I don't recognize the voice."

"I don't either."

"What MC are you with?" she yelled, raising her weapon again.

"Steel Demons! I was their prisoner. I, ah, gave them information..."

"Oh shit," I realized. "It's the guard from the outpost! We've got to get him out."

I ran toward the pile of metal. Noelle set her gun down and followed me.

"What's your name?" I asked the guard.

"Larkan," he answered, followed by a groan of pain.

"We're getting you out, Larkan. Can you tell me where you're pinned? Arms, legs, torso?"

"My shoulder feels fucked," he grimaced. "I kinda feel like I'm holding an entire bike on the back of my shoulders. If I move, it'll crush me completely."

"I can see you," Noelle said, peering through gaps in the pile-up. She looked at me. "How strong are you, Mari?"

"Uh, not strong enough to move a whole bike myself."

She stood up, stuck her fingers into her mouth to let

out a sharp whistle, then waved at her fellow dirt bike riders in the distance. "Hey! We could use some muscle over here!"

A team of four came over, and with careful maneuvering and Larkan talking us through, they were able to lift the bike off of him.

"Don't move," I warned the facedown man with his forearms braced on the ground.

He wore no cut, and his shirt was bloody, covered in dirt and ripped to shreds. It looked like he went skidding with the bike when it went down.

"Your shoulder's dislocated," I observed. "Your other one looks fine, but I have to pop this one back into place. This is going to hurt, okay?"

"Okay," he panted.

"On three. One, two—"

"Ahhh, fuck!"

"Sorry," I told him. "It's better when you're not bracing yourself for it. You can move now, but slowly. Wiggle your toes, fingers, ankles, wrists. Tell me if anything hurts."

Larkan did as I said, checking every major joint gently for any breaks. "Everything hurts but I think I'm okay." He flipped over onto his back, making eye contact with Noelle and I for the first time, and I think we were both taken by surprise.

Even while covered in sand and blood, road rash all over his skin and his shirt hanging off of him in tatters, he was cute. Like, really cute.

His rich brown hair was a few shades lighter than Reaper's, with eyes almost as crystal-blue as Gunner's.

His nose was a little crooked in an endearing way and his smile was pained, but heartfelt.

And it shone straight at Noelle.

"You two just saved my life," he panted.

"That was all her," Noelle waved her hand in my direction, but a nervous smile played at her lips.

I dug through my pack to let them have a small moment, smiling to myself before producing a pill bottle.

"Here, take one of these for the pain. We'll have to clean you up when we get everyone inside the compound. Can you walk?"

"I think so."

"Here," Noelle held an arm out. "Hold onto me."

I swore I saw literal sparks fly when he touched her arm, using it for leverage to pull himself to his feet.

"You're gonna make me lose my man card," he joked, seemingly unable to keep his eyes away from Noelle.

"Your dick still works, doesn't it?" Noelle's mouth dropped open and she slapped a hand over it as if someone else made her say that. "Oh my God, that's so inappropriate! I don't even know you! I'm sorry, the president's my brother and I just—"

"It's all right," Larkan seemed far more amused than offended. "And yes, it does still work. Guess I'll hold onto that man card after all."

Redder than her hair color, Noelle hid her face behind her hands when one of the dirt bike riders waved at us from a nearby crash site.

"Hey! Has anyone seen Reaper?" he called.

"No, why? What did you find?" I rushed over, Noelle's blossoming romance now the farthest thing from my mind.

"Here's his bike," he motioned. "And it's all fucked up."

No. Please, no.

Fucked up was an understatement. The bike looked like a giant tried to fold it in half. Reaper's personal items were strewn out all over the ground, including the gavel which marked his symbol as a leader.

I picked it up slowly, my fingers digging into the grooves of the wood.

"But his body isn't here?" I asked no one in particular.

"No. I think we got everybody except him. There are a bunch of un-ID'd bodies, though—"

"Find him," I demanded.

I didn't know who I was talking to. I wasn't even in a position to give anyone orders. But Reaper, dead or alive, *had* to be found. My body felt like it was going to burst from the inside out without knowing. But if he was one of those mangled, twisted bodies buried under a pile of metal, would I be able to handle *that* knowledge?

"Any sign of Hades?" I asked the dirt bike riders.

One of them pulled off his helmet and I recognized him as Bones, one of the men dating Heather, Reaper's ex.

"No sign of the pooch, either," he told me apologetically. "But if they're out there, we'll find both of them."

I nodded, at a loss for any more words when a hand squeezed my shoulder from behind.

"My brother's like a cockroach," Noelle told me. "Impossible to kill. He's on the wanted lists for at least five surrounding territories. Don't worry, Mari. He'll turn up."

"I hope you're right," I told her.

She gave my shoulder another affectionate squeeze before rubbing the top of my back. "Come on, medic. We've got a long night ahead of us."

She was right. I had to put aside my worries for the man I desperately didn't want to lose. I had to do my job, to focus on the ones who needed me right then and there.

NINETEEN

MARIPOSA

The chaos of the battle's aftermath continued inside the Steel Demons' gates but this time, I was in my element.

Everyone who needed immediate medical attention piled into the clubhouse conference room, where the lights were brightest and people could sit on the tables or chairs as they waited for me.

Those who had stayed home brought water and light snacks to those of us who'd been out in the field. I told Noelle to grab bandages, antibacterial soap, and rubbing alcohol, and clean up people with the minor injuries like road rash. Others helped by keeping pressure on more serious wounds. Meanwhile, I worked from most severe injuries to least. For those in the most pain, I stuck them with local anesthesia and moved on to do something else while waiting for it to kick in. Tessa waddled in just as Big G let out a loud whimper from my syringe.

"Tessie!" he cried out when he saw her. "Baby!"

"Hey, Tess," I gave her a tight smile as I wiped down the skin surrounding the bullet wound. "I'd hug you, but you know..."

She laughed at the sight of my scrubs, already covered with blood even though I quickly changed them from the road. "I'll stay out of your way. We'll reunite later, but I just wanted to see you." She rubbed her husband's back. "And you, I guess."

"Baby, stay with me?" he begged.

"You probably shouldn't stay in here," I warned her. "There are a lot of open wounds here and potential breeding grounds for infection. If you come in contact with anything, it could pose a risk to the baby."

"She's my wife!" Big G yelled. "She stays with me, medic."

"God, shut up," Tessa smacked him. "Don't yell at Mari. She knows more than you." Her eyes lifted to me with a protective hand on her belly. "I'll be in the kitchen, helping with food."

"Tell them lots of vegetables," I said to her. "Especially dark, leafy greens. And hearty soups with bone broth. This lot is going to be out of commission for a while and they'll need good food to recover."

"I'm so glad our boys are in your care," Tessa smiled as she turned to leave. "It's good to have you back, Mari."

I extracted the bullet from Big G's calf and stitched him up without much incident. He apparently didn't have much to say to me without someone else paying attention. I gave him his recovery instructions, then moved on to Jandro who I anesthetized earlier.

"How you holding up?" he asked, leaning over the conference table with his back to me so I could reach his shoulder.

"Better than all of you," I snapped on a pair of fresh gloves and carefully examined his wound.

"We'd be so fucked if it weren't for you," he murmured.

"I dunno. I have a feeling this isn't the first time you've all been in a gunfight."

"Far from it. See that scar on my other shoulder?"

I shined my light on it briefly. "Jesus. The surgeon carved you up."

"Yeah. We used to pile the injured into a truck, drive thirty minutes north to a clinic and pray it would still be open. Then had to threaten the medics at gunpoint to treat us."

"Jesus," I muttered again, not feeling particularly chatty as I worked.

"We paid them in food and basic supplies. But yeah, we've lost a few good Demons over the years. It's part of MC life, but Reaper's been determined to have our own medic. And holy fuck I'm glad we have you, *Mariposita*."

The sentiment was sweet but my work mindset refused to break. I had so much more to do. Flirting with him could wait, but the mention of Reaper's name brought a fresh ache in my chest.

"Has anyone seen him yet?"

"They're out searching right now." He reached over with his good arm to touch my knee. "Not just among the bodies. He might've chased one down that was trying to get away."

"But they found his bike in the rubble."

"He could've hopped on another one." Jandro gave my knee a gentle squeeze. "He'll come back, Mari."

I extracted the metal slug from his shoulder and got to work on his sutures in silence. Focusing on my task was the only thing that kept my hands steady and my heartbeat calm. Every minute that passed without Reaper's presence in his own domain just felt wrong. I saw the worry on everyone else's faces, too. We all wanted to believe he'd come swaggering back through that door, Hades trotting at his side, but what if he didn't? What was this club without its leader?

His gavel felt like a brick in my pocket. I probably wasn't supposed to have it, but it gave me an odd sense of comfort. Like he was still near me.

"How long you gonna be at it?" Jandro asked, pulling me out of my autopilot suturing.

"As long as it takes," I sighed. "Probably all night."

"I'll bring you coffee." His hand never left my knee and now slid up my thigh slightly.

"Thanks."

A twinge on my right side suddenly twisted and cramped. I'd felt some sensation there since getting back but it started getting more intense. My gut, or something within me, told me it had to do with Shadow.

"Has Shadow had his injury looked at?" I asked Jandro.

"He won't let anyone come near him," he sighed. "He gets like this sometimes, like a feral animal. I'll talk him into letting you see him, though."

"Thanks." I snipped the end of my thread after tying

it off and wiped the surrounding skin clean one more time. "I don't think he had but a bad graze but it could get serious if left untreated."

"Leave it to me." He turned toward me, hand still on my thigh, then leaned in like he was going to kiss me.

The conference room door crashing open made me jerk away, partially relieved and disappointed at the interruption.

The search party had returned. Bones and Dallas walked in, grim expressions on their faces as they looked at Jandro.

"What is it?" he asked.

"No sign of Reaper among the bodies. Or Hades," Bones added with a glance toward me.

"So he's still out there," Jandro said confidently. "We'll search out farther in the morning."

Dallas glanced up nervously. "The thing is, some of the crash sites leaked oil and caught fire. When we put them out, the bodies were impossible to identify."

"Then go by the patch on the cut," Jandro snapped. "Did *any* of them have an SDMC patch?"

Bones shook his head. "There are three corpses so badly damaged, we can't ID them by anything. Their clothes literally burned away."

The whole room fell silent. As the information sank into everyone's mind, the worst part was that it told us absolutely nothing. Reaper could be one of those bodies, or he might not be.

"None of those are him," Jandro decided, raising his voice and turning around to look sternly at every-one. "If you didn't find a dog corpse nearby, none of those bodies are Reaper's. Hades never would've left his side."

Bones cleared his throat. "With all due respect," he said hesitantly, "while he's not here, club law says we're to look to you in the interim."

"He'll be here. It's only been a few hours. We don't need to catastrophize this yet."

"Jandro," I whispered.

He looked at me, then down at the gavel I held out in my hands.

"Where did you get that?" he asked.

"It was near his bike. It looked like a hard crash, all his personal stuff was out everywhere."

He closed my fingers over the small, wooden hammer, then gently pushed my hand back toward my body.

"When he shows up, you can give it to him," he smiled. "He'll love that. You two," he snapped to the two men who just walked in. "And everyone else who's not injured. Start cleaning up first thing in the morning. Haul the bikes to my shop. Pick up personal items and supplies and sort them out to their rightful places. We're *not* treating Reaper like he's dead until we have certifiable proof."

Everyone returned to their tasks with a low murmur, myself included. I peeled off my gloves and lathered up my hands with antibacterial soap as Jandro smacked a kiss on my cheek.

"Thanks, Doc," he nuzzled against my face for a moment. "Now, coffee."

I nodded and moved on to my next patient. What else could I do?

Noelle seemed to be cleaning up Larkan's road rash well enough, so I handed her cold packs for his shoulder and left them to continue making their googly eyes at each other.

The night wore on. Jandro brought me at least three cups of coffee while I wrapped sprained ankles, checked for head injuries, changed bandages, and so on. My brain was wired but my body wanted to drop from exhaustion. And that was with everyone stepping up to help. I'd have to express my gratitude one day, when I wasn't so tired.

Every so often I looked to the door. My heart jumped into my throat whenever someone came through, but it was never him.

"Mari," Noelle placed a gentle hand on my shoulder when I dropped into a chair, peeling off what felt like my hundredth pair of gloves. "You need to rest. I'm bringing Larkan back home to keep an eye on his injuries. You coming with us?"

I shook my head. "Jandro's still trying to talk Shadow into letting me see him. And if—*when* Reaper comes in, what if he needs attention right away? I should stay here."

"You're not superhuman, Mari. You're about to crash any second."

The moment she said that, I felt like all my systems were shutting down. "Maybe, but I need to stay here. I could take a nap or something."

"I'll clear off the couch and get you a blanket." She left my side, shooing people out of her way.

I paused for a moment to look around the room. The chaos had died down and most people left with their loved ones to return home. For the first time in hours, I didn't have anything immediately to do. And nothing to distract me from the fact that Reaper still wasn't here.

"Come here, girl," Noelle unfolded a large comforter and pointed to the couch. "Lay down."

I did as she commanded, dead on my feet as I stumbled over.

"Poor thing," Noelle mumbled as she brought the blanket over me. "We gotta take care of our little medic, now that she's caring for all of us."

"We are. At least *I* am." The voice sounded like Jandro but I couldn't be sure. My eyelids were too heavy. The blanket and couch too warm and comfortable.

And I fell into a restless sleep before I knew it. But even during sleep, the fear of never seeing Reaper again haunted me.

MARIPOSA

"Reaper...Reaper!"

"He's not here, honey. I'm sorry."

My eyes snapped open to the familiar green eyes looking at me, but they were the wrong ones. Noelle's red bangs fell across her forehead, her brow pinched tight with concern.

"What do you mean?" I blinked, rubbing my eyes. "Where is he? How long have I been out?"

I swore he was here. I felt his hands on me—strong, possessive, and full of his want. I heard him calling me sugar into my ear. But none of it was real?

"You've been out a couple hours. It's almost dawn." Noelle squeezed my hand.

"And he hasn't come back?"

She shook her head slowly. "I'm getting worried, Mari."

That scared me more than anything. The unshakeable president's sister, who knew him better than anyone, was losing hope.

I sat up and pulled her into a hug. She curled up under the blanket next to me and rubbed my back. She didn't cry. Even now she was trying to be strong.

"Hey, girls."

Jandro came over, sounding exhausted. He picked something up from the couch cushion so he could sit next to me. I saw it was the gavel, which must have fallen out of my pocket as I slept.

"You should be holding that," Noelle said in a small voice.

"No." Jandro placed it back in my lap. "I meant what I said. He's still president until we have proof of otherwise."

"But you're—"

"I'm VP whether he's here or not. I'll act in his stead when he's not and carry out his word when he is. But until we have confirmation that the Steel Demons need a new president, I'm not the one meant to hold the gavel."

"Fuck no, you're not."

All three of our heads snapped to the door, where the man in question strode through with a cocky smirk like he owned the place.

"Reaper!" we all cried out.

"And Hades?" I asked, the panic refusing to subside.

The furry beast ran right up to me, attacking me with a strong, four-limbed hug and tons of puppy licks. I hugged him back, the laughter finally escaping me, but it was the sight of his master I couldn't believe.

"Reaper..." I ran to him, my medic's eye taking in

the dried blood on his clothes, the tatters of his shirt from road rash.

"What happened?" The questions flew out of my mouth in rapid fire succession as my hands inspected him everywhere. "Where did you go? Did you hit your head? Is anything broken?"

"Mari, stop." He took hold of my wrists, pinning me with that green-eyed stare I saw moments ago in my dreams. "I'm okay. Most of this blood isn't mine." His road-rashed palm came to my face, his thumb stroking my cheek gently as his eyes burned with relief, and maybe a touch of regret.

"Forgive me, sugar?"

I pressed my hands against his on my face, not caring about blood or germs, just leaning into the need of his rough touch on me.

"Forgive me?" I whispered. "Again?"

The corner of his mouth ticked up. "Truce."

Like air out of a balloon, all of the fears and anxieties over the past day left me all at once. I went from feeling like my heart would explode with worry to feeling as light as air.

"Fuck." Reaper pulled me in close, one arm around my waist, the other wound in my hair. "I was so worried about you. I knew Jandro would keep you safe but still, if I lost you—"

He cut off his own thought with a hard kiss, rough and desperate like he needed my mouth to breathe. I grabbed the torn edges of his shirt to deepen it even more, pushing my tongue into his mouth. His moan was full of longing as his fist curled into the fabric at my waist.

"Well, seems like you two are on better terms since you left," Noelle laughed.

"We weren't talking again right before this," Reaper chuckled, still gripping my hair and staring at me.

"Jesus, Reap," Noelle rolled her eyes. "Mari is a saint to deal with you."

"She is," he sighed, resting his forehead on mine. "I'm not the easiest person to get along with. But I *want* this, sugar. I'll tell you right now, in front of my sister and the guy who is basically my brother," his eyes flicked up toward Jandro, "in front of my family. I want you to be my woman. Whatever that entails, we'll figure it out. But I swear to you, I'm not chasing tail. I'm not gonna have a wandering eye. I'm done with that. I want *you*, Mariposa."

For a man like Reaper, that was probably the biggest declaration of romance I would get. And coming from him, it was perfect. I believed every word. My first instinct was to jump for joy and confess how much I wanted him, too. How this dull ache in my chest spread throughout my bones every day we didn't speak. That I daydreamed about his pretty eyes, cocky grin, and the ways he pleased me in bed while riding on the back of Jandro's bike.

Speaking of Jandro, he was being extremely quiet during this whole reunion. I knew we passed the line of platonic friendship at some point, and we'd have to address that. I also wanted to ensure history didn't repeat itself again in my relationship with Reaper.

He squeezed my arms gently. "Please say something."

I looked up at him, releasing the edges of his shirt to caress his neck.

"I want you, too," I confessed. "But to make this work, I think we need to hash some things out. We need to make some ground rules on what's okay and not okay, then make sure we stick by them."

"I agree." His fingers curled around mine as he turned his head to kiss my palm. "There's a lot I haven't told you, and that's my fault. I forget that other people didn't grow up in the same culture as Noelle and me." He smiled as he gently lowered my hand. "But hopefully that can wait until Hades and I have a bit of time to recover?"

"I suppose," I sighed jokingly, kissing him one more time before stepping away. "If you're not hurt, you're definitely dehydrated."

"Yeah." Reaper eased himself down on the couch, wincing slightly. "We walked back, about thirteen miles by my estimate."

"From where?" Jandro asked, already filling a bowl of water for Hades. "And why on foot?"

"I crashed into a guy who was trying to knock Shadow off of his bike," Reaper accepted water from Noelle, gulping deeply. "We both got thrown off and went tumbling. Lost our weapons so came down to using fists."

"He's probably one of the un-ID'd bodies out there," Jandro muttered.

"Oh yeah. His lower jaw wasn't attached anymore

when I was done."

Noelle jabbed me with her elbow at my open-mouthed stare. "Get used to it, girl."

"One of his buddies came at me shooting," Reaper continued after more gulps of water. "I ducked behind a crash site, saw one of their own bikes still ridable, so I got on and he gave chase. Next thing I know, Sheol is nowhere in sight."

"Hades was with you the whole time?" The pup had finished drinking his own water and now laid his head in my lap.

"Yeah, poor boy got run ragged. Didn't you?" Reaper stroked his head. "You've never ran like that, huh?" The SDMC leader looked up at us with pride. "He took down two riders himself but the guy on my tail, he was damn slippery."

"Mari took down a couple, too," Jandro cocked his head in my direction.

"Really now?" Reaper's eyes sparkled with glee. "I knew you weren't all sugar and sweetness."

"She needs to work on her aim," Jandro said, then laughed at my glare. "What? It's true! Your shots were a little wide."

"I'll be happy to never shoot a man again," I grumbled. "Yes, they attacked us, but I *killed* someone. That's a big deal to me."

"You'll get used to that, too," Noelle said. "'Cause it'll keep happening. And you'll need to know how to defend yourself."

"We'll teach you the basics," Reaper added. "Then Gunner can teach you fancy shit when he's back."

"He's already teaching me how to swim," I said. "I was able to float on my back at the pool."

"I know," Reaper said with a tone I couldn't place. "I saw you two together."

"I bet he's thrilled that Horus took down a Razor Wire, too," Jandro grinned. "He's probably celebrating right now."

"What?" I knitted my brow.

"The bond," Reaper reminded me. "With a kill that big, Gunner definitely would've felt his divebomb and seen the whole thing from the bird's-eye view."

"Anyway," Noelle waved her hand to catch the guys' attention. "How the hell did you end up walking here?"

"Oh, the gas tank was running on empty. I already figured I wouldn't be able to ride it back, so I decided to crash it."

"You what?" I demanded.

"I know my way around bikes, sugar," Reaper placated me. "I wasn't in danger but the dude chasing did not expect it, that's for sure. I let him crash into me, he flipped over his handlebars and cracked his skull open. I think Hades ate some of his brains."

I looked at the adorable, doe-eyed dog in my lap. "Hades, did you?"

He licked his lips and grinned at me. Everyone laughed at my horrified expression.

"Have I heard it all yet?" I groaned, lowering my forehead to my palm.

"Not even close." Reaper threw an arm around my shoulders and kissed my temple. "Welcome to life as an outlaw, sugar."

MARIPOSA

Noelle and Jandro got Reaper and Hades well fed and hydrated. I cleaned Reaper's minor road rash, which turned out to be the most mild case of anyone I saw that day.

"How did everyone else fare?" he asked me as Hades snored by our feet.

"Some gunshot wounds, sprained ankles and dislocated shoulders, but nothing imminently life-threatening."

"Good," he sighed, visibly relieved as he leaned back on the couch. "And good thing you were here." He placed a hand on my thigh, looking at me affectionately. "You must be exhausted, sugar."

"I took a nap for a little bit. I sure as hell didn't go walking for miles all night."

"Yeah, a day with my feet up sounds great." A twinkle flashed in his eye as he smiled deviously at me. "I owe you a bath that's actually relaxing."

"That sounds amazing," I rested my chin on his shoulder. "I think I'll take you up on that."

"What are we waiting for?" His voice already grew husky, fingers kneading the flesh of my leg. Chances were we wouldn't be making it to the bathtub.

Jandro knocked on the conference room door and walked in just as we got to our feet.

"Shadow's on the patio by the pool," he said. "He kind of retreats to quiet places when there's a lot of commotion, but I think I convinced him you're not going to cut his dick off, or whatever he's afraid of."

"Oh, okay." I had forgotten about him for a moment after being so relieved that Reaper came back. I squeezed the president's hand and looked up at him. "I'll be quick."

"I'll get the bath started." He leaned down for a kiss, sensual and lingering. "Come to my room and meet me in the en suite." He squeezed my waist and whispered possessively, "You're not staying in the guest room anymore."

I smiled and gave him a gentle push to the door. "Go. Don't have too much fun without me."

"Never." He stole one last kiss before heading out into the hallway, Hades right on his heels.

Which left me and Jandro alone.

"I'm fucking glad he's back," he said with a sigh. "Honestly, I don't want the responsibility of being president. He's got his flaws but he's a damn good leader."

"I'm glad, too," I said softly, unsure what else to say. What happened now? Was it going to be awkward between us? Were we just going to pretend we never kissed and never spent a night together?

"I'm happy for you, Mari," he added with a tight smile. "I'm glad you two are going to work it out."

"Jandro—"

"Do you need anything? Shadow knows you're coming. If you're good, I have a bunch of wrecked bikes I need to comb through in the shop."

"Okay. Um, yeah." I returned the tight smile. "I won't keep you. Remember to get some rest. I'll look at your sutures later."

"All right. See you, Mari." He said it warmly but walked off like he couldn't wait to get out of there. And with no kiss or hug, or any contact.

I shook my head at myself as I gathered up some fresh gloves and supplies. *You just got back with Reaper. Jandro was a temporary distraction, but he's a friend.*

It took a moment for me to find Shadow on the patio. He sat on a couch tucked back in a dark corner, nursing a large bottle of liquor.

"Good morning, Shadow," I greeted as I approached him. The sun had just risen over the far end of the pool and looked spectacular.

He didn't return the greeting this time, just watched me warily as he took a swig from his bottle.

"I understand you're not comfortable with women or people in general," I said as I snapped on my gloves. "So I'll make this quick. Sound good?"

Again, no answer. His eyes slid away from me with a wordless grunt which I took to indicate consent.

I pulled a chair over to sit in front of him, while I

laid my tools out on the couch next to him. His eyes widened and he hitched in a breath at the sight of my scalpels.

"I'm going to cut away your shirt," I explained, picking up my scissors. "I need you to not move so as to not agitate the wound, okay?"

Another non-reply followed by a swig of the bottle. I really wished he wouldn't. Alcohol thinned the blood and made bleeding worse, but I wasn't here to lecture him about his coping methods. I picked up the scissors and began cutting up the side of his shirt.

He or Jandro already applied pressure to the wound and soaked up a lot of the blood. The graze cut a long gash between his ribs and his hip. Thankfully, it wasn't very deep. The bleeding had slowed and begun to congeal.

I folded back the two sides of his now-cut shirt to access the wound easily. Rummaging through my stuff, my heart sank when I realized I ran out of rubbing alcohol. Fortunately, being a medic in a war zone taught me there were other methods of sterilizing.

"Can I borrow that?" I pointed to Shadow's liquor bottle, which he seemed very reluctant to part with. "I'm out of rubbing alcohol and I need to sterilize your wound."

He scowled at me but passed the bottle over. I hesitated as I held it over his wound. "This is going to hurt like a motherfucker." He looked off toward the pool, elbow propped on the arm of the couch and his chin in his hand, just waiting for this ordeal to be over with.

You and me both, buddy.

His expression didn't change when I poured the alcohol over his skin. Even the most stoic man would have hissed or grit his teeth or something, but Shadow gave no reaction. He only accepted his bottle back when I held it out to him.

"Stitching you up now," I said, preparing the sutures. "This might hurt, too. I'm sorry, I ran out of local anesthesia."

I got my usual response and got down to work. While the wound was shallow, it extended nearly eight inches long, wrapping around his waist from nearly his stomach to his back. It had to hurt like a bitch but he acted like he didn't even notice it. Frankly, he looked bored.

My hands were on autopilot pulling the surgical thread in and out of his skin, which allowed my eyes to wander slightly across his massive body. He had Jandro's beefcake muscles on a frame taller than Gunner. More pale, faded scars like the ones I saw on his arms criss-crossed up the exposed side of his body, disappearing under the remains of his shirt folded over his chest.

There was no way all of this could be self-harm, though they were clearly shallow cuts made by a sharp implement. Which likely explained why he looked nervous at the sight of my scalpel.

His broad chest rose and fell with deep, even breaths as I worked. The movement was calming, if even hypnotic. If he wasn't so damn intimidating, he'd probably make a great cuddler.

"Almost done here," I said with a handful of stitches left to go. "Then I'll be out of your hair."

Another grunt, another swig of liquor.

"And...done." I snipped the end of my thread. "Just let me put some ointment on this." I unscrewed a tube of Neosporin and dabbed it over the closed wound with a finger. "Come see me if this still looks really red in a couple of days, if you have any fever or weakness, or it's oozing stuff. It's been exposed for a while so your chances of infection are slightly higher than the other guys."

I'd bet my entire medical career he wouldn't willingly come see me, but I still found it important to perform my due diligence.

"I'll give Jandro some of this ointment for both of you to use. Just apply it a couple times a day until it's fully closed." I peeled off my gloves and began cleaning up. "Any questions?"

None, naturally, but it didn't hurt to ask.

"Okay." I stood from the chair and gathered up my supplies. "Let me know if you need anything else."

The absolute last thing I expected was his arm to shoot out and wrap around my waist.

"Whoa, Shadow! What?"

He pulled me across his lap, taking away my balance so I had no choice but to splay across his chest. I braced my hands on his shoulders, utterly bewildered as I stared at him.

"Shadow, what are you—"

My answer came as I heard his pants unbutton and unzip just behind my back. Before I could react, he yanked my scrub pants down, peeling them off my feet, and pulled my bare leg over to straddle him. Naked from the waist down, my bare skin touched his.

It happened so fast and out of nowhere, I could only gape at him. He didn't speak a word or look me directly in the eyes, not even as he reached behind my ass to stroke himself to full hardness. *What the fuck is happening?*

A million questions poured rapidly through my mind as Shadow touched himself almost like I wasn't even there. His hand left my waist, just limp at his side. He seemed so detached, even transactional about this.

I only snapped out of my stupor when I felt his hard cock flex against my ass. His hand returned to my waist only to lift me up so he could—

"Shadow, stop!" I pressed my hands to his biceps. "Wait."

He froze, looking at me directly for the first time. I couldn't read his expression, whether it was angry or confused. He just looked...blank. I said stop, so he did.

But what the ever-loving fuck? Where did this come from? And what would he do if I tried to get away?

His grip on my waist was tight, his strong fingers digging into my skin. Jandro trusted both of us enough to leave us alone—did he ever think this would be happening? He wouldn't let me come alone if he considered Shadow a risk to my safety, would he?

Because even though we were on the same team, Shadow was one big, intimidating motherfucker, and he only ever said two words to me in the weeks I'd been with the club. A memory flashed of him tying me up the first time the Steel Demons took me. He bound me tightly, doing as he was ordered by Reaper, but no one was ordering him now. What would he do to someone smaller and weaker than him with no one watching?

I didn't *want* to think the worst but here I was with my pants down, in the last situation I expected after Reaper and Gunner assured me their men didn't prey on women. The fact of the matter was I didn't know anything about Shadow, aside from his strong disdain of women and that he was an experienced, skilled killer.

In my panicked, utterly confused state of mind, it seemed the best course of action was to give him what he wanted.

So I raised my hips and reached behind me, feeling for the cock he was just about to shove into me with nothing leading up to it. No foreplay, no flirting, not even a word exchanged. And fuck me, it was huge.

My fingers nearly didn't touch as they wrapped around the shaft. Shadow's hand fell away from my waist, his eyelids softening at the contact of my hand on him. It seemed he wasn't bothered about putting in any effort once he saw that I was about to take the reins.

I can't believe I'm fucking doing this. Reaper is waiting for me in his fucking bathtub for fuck's sake! I screamed in my head.

Shadow's fists curled at his sides when I swept the crown of his dick against my entrance. Just that motion squashed any thoughts about running off. A single swing from one of those fists would send my brain matter all over the patio. The consequences of this would be grave but no one was coming to my rescue now, and I just had to get through it.

Lowering myself onto him was a slow, arduous process with his size and the complete lack of foreplay but I found myself wetter than I expected, given the circumstances. He was, after all, the first of the four sexiest Demons I really noticed. Reaper was the first one I *saw*, but it was Shadow who made me bump into his coffee table when I came over to serve him beer.

The tall, imposing frame, those tortured, soulful eyes, and all the scars he tried to keep hidden. He clearly had no idea how magnetizing that was to some women. To touch him was not only to flirt with danger, but to fall into it unabashedly. Even now, in this situation, my palm itched to touch the short beard covering his jaw, to push away the long hair he kept over his face so he'd look at me with both eyes.

But if I did, would I live to tell about it?

His head tilted back with a soft hiss as his length began disappearing inside me. I found myself doing the same as he stretched me out from the inside. The sensation was intense, but not painful. When I began a slow roll of my hips, my hands splayed out to brace myself for leverage. My fingers met the bare skin of his abdomen, his cut T-shirt now falling away to the side.

With my knees on the couch cushions on either side of his thighs, I found a somewhat steady rhythm as I rode him. He never touched me or made a sound. His eyes flicked up and down, from where our bodies connected, to where my hands rested on him, to my still fully-clothed torso hovering above him, but he never met my eye.

He was so…cold. Clinical and detached. Men who paid for whores showed more enthusiasm than this.

That thought process only spiraled back to the pervasive question of *why* did he start this?

I tried to act the same way he did. Not making a sound, not looking at him, not doing anything but the bare minimum to get him off so I could end this and run to Reaper. But I could never treat sex that way, not even like this.

And I couldn't ignore the fact that he was a fucking specimen of a man. Beautiful in such a sad, dark way. Massive arms and chiseled shoulders I just wanted to run my hands across. The Steel Demons skull emblem sat inked on the left side of his chest, right over his heart. I wanted to trace it with my fingers like I did with Reaper's. Or maybe with my tongue.

I became so entranced with all the fine details of his body, I didn't notice the moan escaping my mouth until it was too late. For once, he looked up at my face, surprised. And my face burned red with shame at the realization that I was *enjoying* this.

He was hot as hell, with a huge dick that stretched me in ways I didn't know were possible. And yes, he was dangerous and a cold blooded killer, but he wasn't forcing me to do anything. I probably had the advantage at this point to hop off and run for my life, but I didn't *want* to.

My hands skimmed up his abs to his chest, splaying open my fingers wide to *feel* the heat of his skin, the beat of his heart under that grinning skull. I rode him even more vigorously, taking the full length of him on every downstroke and moaning openly each time he filled me.

Still he didn't say a thing, or move his hands from his

sides to touch me. I had so many questions, so many ways I wanted to test him with small gestures. How would he react to a kiss? Or if I just grabbed his hands and put them on me?

But as much as I enjoyed him, his complete lack of reaction also made me insecure. This could still end badly for me if I pushed things too far. I just didn't know him well enough to take that risk.

So I settled for caressing him, enjoying the view and feel of him as I rolled my hips back and forth. He let out a sigh as my hands reached his chest again, then his whole body stiffened with a groan.

A moment later I felt the swelling and spilling of warmth as he released inside me. He panted as I slowed my movements, and then I felt the first touch with the tiniest glimpse of intimacy—his fingers brushing against my knee.

And like that, I felt like a blindfold had been torn away from my eyes.

Fuck.

Fuck!

Oh fuck, what did I just do?

I pressed on his chest with my hands to swing my leg over, wobbling like a newborn giraffe as I grabbed my pants and made my best attempt to insert my legs.

Once dressed, I grabbed my supplies and walked away without a word or even a glance at the man behind me.

TWENTY-TWO

REAPER

Holy mother of cunt balls, my whole body fucking hurt.

Motorcycle boots were not made for thirteen-mile long walks so not only were my feet killing me, my knees, hips, and back were feeling about eighty years old, too. But I didn't get any fresh bullet holes or road rash or cactus spines in my dick today, so at least there was an upside.

Hades and I limped home to find Fischlin's guard on one of my couches, wearing nothing but one of *my* pairs of sweatpants and a bag of frozen peas on his shoulder. To add insult to injury, his feet were also propped up on *my* mahogany coffee table I stole from a governor's vacation home.

"The fuck you doin' in my house?" I asked.

"He's with me."

The answer came from Noelle, who just emerged from the linen closet with a folded blanket and a pillow.

"Excuse me?" I asked.

"I said, he's with me." She dropped the blanket and pillow on the couch next to him, then faced me with her hands on her hips.

Oh hell. I hated when my sister got sassy.

"And what the fuck do you mean by that?"

"You bring home strays, I take care of them. Just the way it's always been."

"And you gave him *my* pants?"

"Well, he won't fit into mine!"

"Hey, hey, it's all right." The guy gave an uneasy smile as he stood up, hands raised in a de-escalating manner. "Reaper, uh, Mr. President, I appreciate you bringing me along with your club after everything that happened. I don't want to impose so if you'd rather not have me in your house, I can stay somewhere else."

"No, Larkan, it's fine," Noelle insisted. "Reaper's grumpy as hell on his best days, so he's bound to be a little moody after his trek through the desert."

"Noelle," I sighed, pinching the bridge of my nose. "Just…come here a minute."

I limped over to my study—Goddamn, I was dying to get off my feet—and closed the door after my sister followed me in.

"What the hell is going on?" I asked, folding my arms.

"What? Nothing." She matched my posture. "It's like I said. First Hades, then Mari, now Larkan. You bring home strays, I give them a home. Same as always."

"No," I shook my head. "This one's different."

"What do you mean?" Her voice went a little high on the last word.

"Are you just looking to get laid or is it something more?"

"Reaper!" she growled. "That's not what this is!"

"Yeah, right. He's a grown-ass man whose mechanic skills rival Jandro's and he's a sharpshooter. We're gonna integrate him as a prospect and see how he does. He doesn't *need* to be taken care of. But," I flashed her a taunting smile, "he does have a six-pack and pretty eyes, doesn't he?"

"Fuck you," she punched my arm. "Why would I set him up on the couch if I wanted to get laid?"

"Hence the other part of my question. Is it something more?"

"I literally just met the guy! You all kept him prisoner and never bothered to learn his name as you grilled him for information. Where else would he go? Maybe I'm just trying to be fucking nice? You know, like I was when you dragged Mari out here against her will!"

"Whatever. I'm too fucking tired to argue about this." I scrubbed a hand down my face with a sigh. "Just don't get involved with him, Noelle. That's an order from your president, not your older brother being protective."

"Hah!" she scoffed, raising both of her hands. "You are *way* jumping the gun, tiger."

"I mean it," I growled. "He's given us good intel, but we still don't know if he's loyal enough to be a Demon. And we—" I stopped myself, before choosing to go on with a sigh. "We've had a breach of trust among our own. I'll fill you in later, but this attack was orchestrated by General Tash. He has, for all intents and purposes, turned against us and declared war on us, based on information someone in the club has been feeding him."

"What?" Her mouth dropped open, for once speechless. "Who would do that?"

"I'm not sure," I admitted. "But whoever it is will fucking regret it."

———

A HOT BATH was just what I needed. Soaking up to my armpits, I puffed on a cigar next to the open window and sipped from a glass of my favorite whiskey. The only thing that would've made it better was my sweet little medic snuggled up against me. She was taking her sweet ass time but maybe Shadow's injuries were more extensive that she originally thought.

I puffed and exhaled, closing my eyes to lean my head back against the cool tile. I couldn't pussyfoot around it this time. She had to know not only my intentions, but the reasoning behind them. Best case scenario, she'd embrace it and be thrilled. Worst case, it would just be me and her.

And I was honestly fine with that. If she wanted me to be her only man, I'd do everything in my power to be everything she needed. It was all I thought about on my long trek back home.

Just my luck that the first woman I considered worthy of sharing balked at the first mention of it. Most women outside of my family's culture thought it was some culty brainwashing shit and I didn't give a fuck. I was fine to fuck them and ride off the next day anyway. They'd never get the irony of a one-night stand between two people, while completely dismissing the intimacy and trust between a woman and her harem.

But I desperately wanted Mariposa to understand. And if she didn't go for it, then I would try my best to understand where she was coming from.

That's what people did when they fell in love, right?

"Mari's here!" Noelle called from downstairs.

"Then get that sweet ass up here!" I returned.

"She's getting a robe out of my room!" Noelle reported.

"Fuck that, I want her naked!"

I chuckled to myself, puffing on my cigar, then cringed and coughed. I did not want to think about what Noelle was doing with that guy downstairs, nor did I want to give her any ideas.

Ah, whatever. My woman was here.

"There you are." I leaned back in the tub as Mari's bare feet padded over the tiled floor. "Almost thought the water would get cold before you got here."

"Sorry," she mumbled, slipping the robe off her shoulders and letting the fabric pool on the floor.

I didn't get a chance to enjoy the view. She looked away from me as she climbed in, settling between my legs with her bare back as stiff as a board. Aside from her hips brushing my thighs, she made no move to touch me. She stayed hunched over, knees drawn up and arms against her chest.

That was fucking weird.

I lifted my hand from the water with a small splash, moving her hair from her back to the front of her shoulder. Then I circled my thumb against her upper back, working the stiff muscles until she released a soft sigh. Taking hold of her shoulder, I pulled back gently and she followed until her back rested on my chest.

I moved the massage to her upper arms, letting the water trickle over her skin to aid in her relaxation. Dragging my lips along the back of her neck, I pressed a kiss to the soft spot behind her ear.

"What's wrong, sugar?"

Her heartbeat and her breathing accelerated. I waited, despite the urge of demanding the truth from her. It had been a long time since I comforted a woman who was more than just a casual fuck, but I did my best. My hands ran up and down her arms and I dropped more kisses on her neck and shoulder.

"I had sex with Shadow."

All my movements paused. The words tumbled out of her in a hurried confession, and her heart thumped erratically through her back.

"Okay." That was the last thing I expected to hear come out of her mouth. Shadow hadn't occurred to me as someone to share her with, mainly because he didn't seem interested in most normal things, least of all women.

"I didn't want to at first," she breathed in the same hurried, verging-on-panicked fashion. "I said stop and he did, but...I didn't know what he would do next, so I just…kept going until he finished."

"Wait." My own heart now crashed erratically as I

grabbed her shoulder again and turned her so she faced me. "Are you saying *Shadow* forced himself on you?"

"It all happened so fast," her lip wobbled. "I finished cleaning his wound and then he's holding me in his lap and pulling my pants down. I stopped it before anything actually happened, but then I..." Her eyes lifted to mine, wet with tears. "I didn't expect to feel like shit, but I—"

"Mari, was there *anything* you could have said that made Shadow think you wanted to? He won't even be in the same room as a woman if he can help it, let alone fuck one against her will."

"I don't know." Two fat tears tracked down her cheeks. "I don't even know why I'm so upset. I was scared at first but now I feel like...I cheated on you—"

"You didn't cheat on me," I scoffed. "What we have is not some outdated bullshit like that." *Fuck.* I bit my tongue too late. So much for understanding where she was coming from.

"Right." She wiped her tears away forcefully. "That's right, Reaper. I know you don't do traditional relationships."

"Don't put words in my mouth, Mari," I warned. "I haven't told you what that means so don't make assumptions about me." Then in my best attempt at a gentler voice I added, "This is how we end up fighting, remember?"

"I'm sorry. I just...I'm so confused." Her eyes were gigantic and pained as they met mine. But *she* wasn't pained, I realized. She thought she hurt *me*.

"Come here," I pulled her toward my chest. "I'm

not angry and I don't blame you for this. I mean it, sugar. You haven't done anything wrong by me."

"How can you say that?" Her arms went around my neck. "I just slept with another man right after we agreed to work on us!"

"Mari, look at me." I wrapped one arm around her back and held her chin in the other hand. "Do you still want to be with me?"

"Yes," her breath fanned over my lips and I ached to kiss her. "Of course I do. But how can you—"

"That's all that matters to me," I told her. "You care enough to come straight here and tell me. You still want to be the woman at my side." I dragged my thumb across the tear resting on her cheekbone. "You're honest. You're loyal. And you're mine. There's no reason for you to feel so guilty about this."

"I do, anyway." She let out a shuddering sigh. "I can't believe I let it happen. I never want to be in that situation again."

"Come here." I pulled her in until her thighs wrapped around my waist and her arms encircled my shoulders.

My hands pressed up and down into her back in an effort to soothe her. I dropped kisses to her shoulder as she buried her face in my neck. All the while, I tried to rationally process what she told me. Why wasn't Jandro with her? Shadow only had sex with whores. What made him think she wanted it, when the aftermath clearly showed she didn't? And yet, it didn't sound like he raped her.

I pressed a kiss to her ear before asking, "Did he hurt you?"

"No. He didn't…*do* anything besides start it. It was all me. I guess that's why I feel like shit."

I waited a few moments before asking my next question.

"Did you enjoy it?"

She let out a soft gasp and jerked away from me like I hit her, her face crestfallen.

"I swear to God, Reaper. I don't know where I stand with you. First you're wiping my tears away, then you want to know sordid details like—"

"You want to know where you stand with me?" I pointed to the left side of my chest. "Right fucking here."

Her mouth snapped shut as she swallowed, starting at where my finger pressed directly to my heart.

"Now you're the medic, so correct me if I'm wrong," I continued, "but this organ is not the same thing as my dick."

She huffed out a soft laugh and a smile for the first time since entering the room. "No, you're right." Her eyes lifted up to mine and it looked like something clicked. "So what are you saying?"

"I'm saying sexual or even emotional monogamy is not a requirement for me in a partner. But," I lifted a finger to stop her from saying anything else, "in the culture I grew up in, only women were privy to this. I had one mom and three dads, remember?"

"You mean your dads were *only* with her and no one else?"

"Yeah. All three of them were completely devoted to her." I stared blankly at the water's surface as childhood memories filtered through my head.

"It never felt…I dunno, unfair?"

"Not at all. It was a beautiful, sacred thing cherished by everyone involved." My gaze returned to hers. "There were rules to it, though. Our society was a bit complex. Technically you broke a rule but that's okay." I directed a small splash at her to show I was joking. "You didn't know. And it's nowhere near as bad as cheating."

"So," she looked apprehensive, but not as crushed as a few minutes ago. "You want to have that kind of relationship with me?"

"Only if it's something you want, too." I grabbed her waist and pulled her back once again to straddle me. "I'll explain it later, lay it all out for you. Then you can think about it and decide if it's something you want to try. If not," I sucked in a breath, "I'll try my damndest to be good enough for you as your only man. I *don't* want other women, I'm not wired that way. But if you're only with me…sugar, I'm gonna piss you off. I'm probably gonna hurt your feelings again, even though I don't mean to."

Mari laughed lightly, running her fingers over my scalp as her forehead touched mine. "I have a feeling that's gonna happen regardless if it's just you or not."

"You're probably right." My hands molded to the curves in her back again. "Just hear me out before you write it off?"

"I can do that." She smiled against my lips before

bringing a fist to her mouth to stifle her yawn. "Later, though?"

"Later," I promised, kissing her after she finished yawning. "Rest first. And I gotta hold church to bring everyone up to speed. I'm sure you'll have patients to check on."

"Yeah…" Her eyelids were already drooping as she leaned on me.

"And hey," I kissed her forehead.

"Hm?"

"I'll find out what happened," I told her. "And I'll make sure it doesn't happen again."

———

MARI and I slept from the ass-crack of dawn all day until the following afternoon. When we got up, she made her rounds checking on patients while I poured over some work in my study. Just to make her feel safer, I told Hades to go with her, which he seemed *very* happy about.

That evening, I found Jandro and some other guys drinking and playing cards around the fire pit next to the pool.

"One of you fuckers pour me something and deal me in. You," I pointed at Jandro, "I need a word. Alone."

His eyebrow popped up in surprise. "Sure thing, Reap."

He followed me into the clubhouse and through the hall until we reached the church conference room, neither of us saying a word until I locked the door behind us.

"What's going on?" Jandro's tone was cool, but brimmed with curiosity.

I huffed out a breath. "You need to find out from Shadow *exactly* what the hell happened after Mariposa treated him."

Jandro's eyes narrowed as he crossed his arms. "Wha—"

"She's saying he fucked her." The words came out with a growl, whether out of jealousy or protection, I couldn't be sure. "And she came to me right after, all upset."

"What, fucked her? You mean like actual…?" He made an O-shape with his hand and stuck his opposite index finger through to demonstrate.

"Yes, Jandro. That is generally what people mean by fucking."

"You can't be serious." He looked baffled. "This is *Shadow* we're talking about."

"I know. It makes no sense to me either." I scrubbed a hand down my face. "But Mari's not lying about this. She was all quiet, then she started crying—"

"You don't think—" Jandro cut himself off abruptly, jerking his eyes away for a moment before looking back at me. "Reap, no. Shadow wouldn't."

"That's why I'm telling you to find out what happened. He'll say more to you than anyone else."

"He's never hurt anyone in this club, you realize that?" my VP asked me intently. "He's never even showed up to a Fight Night. Reaper, she must've—"

"Don't say it," I warned him. "Don't you fucking say she wanted it to happen. She said it felt like *cheating* on me."

"Fuck me, man," he sighed heavily. "You still haven't told her?"

"I started to," I said. "She gets the basic idea but we haven't talked about it in depth yet." I cut my hand through the air. "Doesn't fucking matter, anyway. She did *not* want this to happen. And it will *not* be repeated, you hear me?"

"Yeah, man. I got it."

"So what the hell are you waiting for?" I snarled when he just kept fucking standing there.

"Shadow turned in early tonight. He's probably already asleep."

"Then wake his ass up."

"And get thrown across the room like a rag doll? No thanks," he huffed. "I'll talk to him in the morning."

"See that you do." I headed for the door. "I want two apologies—one to me, for having my woman without permission, and one directly to Mari—"

"Reap, dude," Jandro gave me a pleading look. "You know how he is—"

"—for upsetting the woman who saved all your lives." I opened the door. "That'll be all, Jandro."

I left him there, heading back to the patio where a card game, a drink, and a fat cigar waited for me. Sure, I knew exactly how Shadow was and tolerated it up until now. He was a loyal soldier and a damn good assassin. He didn't have to morph into a chatty Cathy but shit had to change from here on out. He needed to know

Mariposa wasn't some whore to paw at. Hell, every Steel Demon needed to know it, but he especially needed it drummed through that thick skull.

She deserved to walk among us feeling safe and respected.

Because she was mine.

TWENTY-THREE

JANDRO

"Chela, Perdita, Letty, Foghorn," I sighed, tugging on the string I just tied to make sure it was secure. "I swear you guys are the only ones *not* being a pain in my ass lately."

The girls just clucked as they pecked at the head of cabbage I strung up for them as a treat. Foghorn was chilling by the workout bench, nice and quiet after crowing at all ungodly hours of the night. That made my next-door neighbor, Big G and his family, less than thrilled. But I begrudgingly got them on board with my new pets after promising fresh eggs once the girls started laying.

Truthfully, though, with Reaper breathing down my neck about what Shadow did, Mariposa forgetting my existence since her man was back, piles of fucked up bikes in my shop, and *still* dealing with a betrayer in our club, hanging out with chickens seemed like a fine idea.

I watched them peck at the head of cabbage while

enjoying my coffee in a deck chair. Foghorn decided to see what his ladies were fussing about and walked over with his dinosaur-like gait.

I sighed. If only sharing food was the biggest of my problems. I didn't expect it to nag at me so much that Mari and Reaper got back together so quickly. We all feared the worst for him, and I could only imagine how he felt leaving his woman in the midst of a battle.

My heart didn't hurt. It didn't even sting, really. I just missed her.

I felt like a fallback guy, the one she went to when things were rough with her main squeeze. When did that happen? Never before had I ever let a woman yank me around. I knew all the tricks in the book. Crocodile tears and pouty lips had no effect on me.

Who was I kidding? I knew Mari wasn't being manipulative and it was wrong trying to paint her that way. She was just doing her best to navigate her feelings in a world that was completely foreign to her.

And now this whole thing with Shadow threw me for one hell of a loop. I thought for sure Reaper was fucking with me, but the dude was fuming. Now I had to put on my dad-pants *again* and get everyone to make up. Just great.

I heard the sliding glass door whoosh open behind me, signaling that Shadow had risen and was coming outside for his workout.

"Mornin'," I greeted without looking at him.

I got a grunt in reply, then watched him grip the horizontal bar to begin his pull-ups.

The man worked out religiously every morning we were at home. He was shirtless and with his hair tied back. Only in this yard and in present company was he ever comfortable doing so. I'd bet my flock of chickens I was still the only person who saw his face unobstructed.

I lost count of his pull-ups around sixty. He did about twenty more before grabbing a 45-pound plate to hold between his ankles and began another set.

I could hardly believe I was looking at the same skinny, malnourished and timid kid curled up into a ball at my prison job so many years ago. With plenty of food and a set of heavy weights to lift, he turned into a beast.

Or rather, he was always a beast. Now he was just no longer caged.

"Your stitches look good, Frankenstein," I called out, noticing the clean, sutured wound just above his hip.

My shoulder was sore as hell from the gunshot wound, but I hadn't broken out in a fever this time. Mari must have done a good job of preventing infection from spreading.

Shadow didn't respond to my comment, but began his next set. Even with me, he chose not to say anything unless he had to. I was stalling and knew it was useless. Reaper would have my balls if I didn't get to the root of the matter *today*.

Time to rip the band-aid off.

"Can I talk to you for a minute, bro?"

"Yes," he grunted out between his hand-clap push-ups.

I drained the rest of my coffee and put it down

beside me, knowing he'd want to finish his current set before talking.

He did fifteen more then rose up to standing, breathing with a bit of effort but otherwise not looking at all like he just completed a workout that would kill most men. And that was just his warm-up.

"What would you like to talk about?"

Even though we were friends and I trusted the guy with my life, he looked intimidating as hell walking across the yard toward me. The sun made him squint, adding more tension to his already permanently scowling face. The morning's brightness also turned his pupils to pinpricks, exaggerating the contrast between his brown eye and his white eye.

I blew out a breath. "Have a seat, man."

He cocked his head at me but relented, lowering himself down to sit on the deck next to my chair.

"What happened after Mariposa stitched you up the other night?"

"We fucked."

I groaned and raised a hand. "Okay, back it up a notch. *How* did that happen?"

"She offered and I accepted."

"What do you mean, she *offered?* What exactly did she say?"

"She said, 'let me know if you need anything else.' It *has* been over six months since you sent a woman to me, so—"

"Oh my God, Shadow," I groaned, slapping both palms to my face. Fucking fuck sticks, this was my fault.

"Dude, *this* is why I said you need to spend more time around people."

"I don't like people."

"I know, but ugh..." I rubbed my temples, trying to cool my shit. I should have fucking seen this coming but had so much other shit on my mind at the time, my own feelings for Mari included.

Shadow frowned, now apparently clued in to my reaction. "Did I do something wrong?"

"Yeah, man. You kinda did." I looked at him squarely, knowing that telling him straight was more effective than beating around the bush. "I sent her to you *just* to heal you. That is the service she provides, not sex. She's not a whore. She was offering you more medical attention if you needed it."

"Oh."

"Yeah, *oh*," I sighed. "She didn't expect or want to have sex with you. So she was pretty upset afterward—"

"Why?"

I groaned again, returning my hand to my forehead. Talking to him was like talking to a toddler sometimes.

"Because she barely knows you and had no warning it was coming. On top of that, she's Reaper's woman. At this point, he's the only man she's agreed to fuck. Make sense?"

"I guess so." He still looked puzzled.

"I'm not mad at you, dude. I'm just trying to help you understand," I said. "A lot of these things are implied and not explicitly said. If you spend more time in mixed company, men *and* women, you'll pick up on these things and avoid misunderstandings."

"I'm confused because," he scratched at his beard, "she didn't seem upset. She rode me herself. She was moaning and touching me here," he skimmed a hand across his chest. "No other woman has done that before. It made me come faster."

"Okay, I did *not* need to know that," I groaned. "But yeah, women who don't provide sex as a service treat it differently. Most of them only do it with people they care about. So there's more touching, kissing, little things like that. It creates intimacy."

"It felt good. I mean, it always does. But good in a different way." Shadow's hand rested on his chest tattoo, eyes unfocused as he seemed to recall the sensation.

"Well enjoy that memory because it's all you'll ever have," I said. "Reaper ordered me to tell you it's to never happen again. He also wants an apology from you for having his woman without permission."

Shadow's hand dropped from his chest, his eyes going from dreamy to stoic. "Okay. I can do that."

I sucked in a breath. "He also wants you to apologize to Mariposa."

His gaze snapped up to mine, wide-eyed and panicked. "I can't."

"You can and you will," I told him in my most stern dad voice. "You had your dick inside her. You can say you're sorry."

He shook his head. "I can't do it, Jandro."

"Dude, you're a three-hundred pound gorilla. She's *one* little woman. What's the worst she can do to you?"

He looked away without an answer but I saw the tremor in his hands.

I felt awful for the guy. He came such a long way since I found him but his trauma and his fears still ran deep. At least twice a week, all his progress seemed to reset due to his night terrors. Shadow was a beast feared almost more than the Steel Demons name itself. But no one else saw the man trembling in the center of a bedroom filled with furniture torn to splinters, wearing the face of a terrified kid I found in a prison cell.

"I keep telling you most women are *not* like your family," I said in a gentler tone, clapping my hand on his shoulder. "I can tell you until I'm blue in the face, but this is your chance to see it for yourself."

He still didn't answer and I knew he was off somewhere in his head.

"Hey," I snapped my fingers in front of his face. "Stay with me, dude. You're building this up in your head and it's really not that big a deal. You can do this."

"Do I have to?" Jesus, he really was like a child. "I'll apologize to Reaper and he can tell her—"

"No. He was very specific, Shadow. You need to tell her yourself." I sighed. "I know it's scary, man. I used to be terrified of talking to girls, too."

"You were?"

"Like twenty years ago, but yeah. It gets easier the more you do it, though. Trust me on that."

He sighed, resigned to his fate. "Will you help me with what I should say?"

"Sure thing, buddy." I slapped his back. "We'll work it out before church. Get on back to your workout."

He jumped up and returned to the weights like he couldn't wait to get away from this conversation. I, too, was glad to have it over with. Now if only I could get the image of Mari riding his dick out of my head.

A chuckle escaped me despite myself. Shadow had to be the only person in the world who found it easier to cut a man's throat than say a single word to a woman.

TWENTY-FOUR

MARIPOSA

"Ow! Fuck!"

I ignored Big G's complaints as I ripped the bandage off of his bullet wound.

"Ow, that was my fucking leg hair!"

"Oh my God, will you quit your bitching?" Tessa waddled over to the couch while I bit my lip to hold in the laughter.

"You've never been shot, woman!"

"And you've never pushed an eight-pound baby out of your body, so shut the hell up."

She lowered herself on the couch carefully, holding her belly. "Sorry about him, Mari. Don't let it deter you."

"It's all right," I applied more antibacterial ointment to the sutures. "I really do hope Gunner comes back soon so I can get some local anesthesia again."

I finished with her husband and sent him off limping and whimpering. The moment he was gone, I scooted closer to her with my stethoscope and a huge grin on my face.

"How's my favorite little man or lady doing?" I asked, holding the diaphragm end to her belly.

"I swear he's got a fucking motorcycle in there already," she sighed. "Running nonstop."

"Yeah? You thinking boy then?"

"I keep saying *he* but I don't really know." She looked at me longingly. "Can't believe they used to have those machines where you could *see* the baby and everything, all the little parts, too!"

"The teaching hospital at my nursing school had one," I told her. "The really advanced one where you could see everything in 3D. You could watch them suck their thumbs in there, kicking and flailing around, little boys playing with their willies."

"Sounds like my two boys," she laughed before turning serious. "Is it bad to want another boy, Mari?"

"Not at all. You know what to expect, right? Since you already have two."

"Yeah, it's not just that, though." She chewed her lip nervously.

I pulled the ear pieces out and let the stethoscope hang around my neck. "What's wrong?"

"I'm just scared to raise a girl in a world like this," she whispered.

"Oh, honey." I grabbed her hand and squeezed. "She'd have all these big scary men to protect her. Don't tell me the Steel Demons wouldn't kill for a little princess."

"They would," she gave a strained smile. "Dallas and

Andrea's daughter is treasured by everyone here. But her options are so limited as she grows up, unlike for the men. She either stays within the gates of Sheol her whole life or goes out into the world. And what's out there for her? Nothing but a life of slavery."

"I hear you," I said with a nod. "I can't imagine having that kind of fear for my own child. But you know what I think?"

"Hm?"

"We need more women out in the world. To hide them away only creates a demand for them as commodities. We need women in positions of power, in educated jobs, in supportive and leadership roles. That's how we make the world a safer place for our kids."

Tessa gave me a nod and a gentle smile. "I agree with what you're saying. Really, I do. It's just that," she placed a hand on her belly, "it's going to take lots of time and sacrifice to get to that point. And what mother wants to send her children out to be sacrificial lambs?"

I didn't have an answer for her.

————

I FINISHED CHECKING on my patients a bit later that night. The only house I didn't stop by was Jandro and Shadow's.

With Hades at my side, I probably would have been fine. I certainly wouldn't mind seeing Jandro, I even missed him. It was Shadow I was unsure about, so I thought it best to avoid it.

On the way back to Reaper's, we passed by what I

assumed to be Gunner's dark, empty house. I let out a sigh at the thought of the sweet, angel-faced Demon. I missed him, too. Just another man in the carousel to send my head spinning.

Hades howled softly as we walked by, which was answered by a soft screech coming from the house's direction.

"Saying goodnight to your buddy?" I asked, scratching between his ears.

He licked my hand in response.

We walked into the house to the sound of Noelle and Larkan talking in the kitchen. The space was open and covered in marble and stainless steel, so their voices echoed despite talking at a normal volume. It sounded like they were trying to bake something.

Noelle suddenly shrieked which turned into uproarious laughter. Larkan chuckled softly and said something like, "I told you not to touch that."

Those two were nothing if not love at first sight. I smiled all the way to Reaper's study.

"What are you happy about?" he said the moment I stepped into the room.

He sat at the end of a long table similar to the one in the conference room. Papers were strewn out in front of him, a lamp emitting cozy yellow light throughout the room. The president wasn't wearing his cut, but the top three buttons of his henley shirt were undone. His green eyes looked predatory in the warm light and a glass of whiskey completed the ensemble.

"Noelle," I answered, making my way toward him. "She seems so happy."

"Ugh, don't remind me of *that*," he groaned as he stretched his arms above his head. "And here I thought you were happy to see me."

"I am." I leaned over to kiss him, which ended up being futile since he just pulled me into his lap and dominated my mouth. "And what's wrong with your sister being happy?" I asked when I broke away.

"She's going to get her fucking heart broken, that's what's wrong," he grumbled, taking a pull of whiskey. "Noelle is either all in or all out. She doesn't do anything in between. And that guy," he nodded his head toward the door, "I don't trust. Not until he proves himself loyal. And even then, it doesn't mean he's good for her."

"Why not just let her enjoy it?" I pushed his hair back with my fingers before lacing my hands around his neck. "And if it doesn't work out, at least he made her happy for a while."

"Noelle can't just have fun," he sighed. "When she gets her sights on someone, she falls hard and fast. When it ends, she completely breaks down and I have to pick up the pieces." He downed the rest of his whiskey. "She swears she'll never love another man again, then she gets lonely and the cycle repeats."

"She's never had, you know, like your mom and dads?" I'd been thinking of what he told me about his family for most of the day.

"A harem?" He shook his head. "Nah. Unfortunately, her trysts don't really last long enough for multiple relationships to be built, let alone one."

He set his glass down and wrapped both arms

around my back, pulling me forward on his lap until his lips met my neck.

"Enough about my sister," he murmured before kissing the spot between my neck and shoulder. "How's my lover?"

I smiled against his ear, squirming a little from his stubble tickling my skin. "Good. No one's injuries got worse, which is a huge relief. I just didn't check Jandro and Shadow, though. I don't know if you..."

"I took care of it," he kissed me again. "Jandro talked to him and reported back to me. It sounds like it was a misunderstanding, which is kind of what I figured."

"A misunderstanding?"

"Yeah." Reaper leaned back, resting his hands on my thighs. "Shadow doesn't interact with people much, as I'm sure you've seen. Even less so with women. Pretty much the only female contact he's had is with service girls Jandro buys for him."

"Really? His whole life?"

Reaper nodded. "From birth until he met Jandro, he was kept very isolated. He didn't really learn social cues and appropriate behavior until after they met."

"He's covered in scars," I recalled the sight of his arms and torso. "Scars that look old."

Reaper nodded slowly. "The few interactions he had with people growing up were not positive, to say the least."

"Damn," I breathed. "Neurology is not my field, but I can only imagine what that does to someone's brain development."

"You're sexy when you talk medic nonsense," he teased, earning a swat on the chest from me. "Anyway, Shadow will make a full apology to you and me soon. I expect sometime before or after church tomorrow."

"You?" I asked. "What's he apologizing to you for?"

Reaper's hands slid up my thighs, reaching around to grab my ass with both hands. Heat and a dangerous possessiveness filled his eyes.

"Because he had what's mine."

Good lord, I didn't want to find that so hot but I did. It was the perfect opportunity to ask more about his whole sharing thing, but the blood rushing from my head to my sex made me stupid.

"Hm?" It was apparently so hot I zoned out on Reaper asking me a question.

His smirk made me even hotter. "I said, is that acceptable to you? An apology from him?"

"Yeah, I think so. It seems a bit," I thought for a moment, "a bit cruel, even. If talking to women in particular makes him so uncomfortable."

"A fitting punishment, then," Reaper said. "He's not afraid of anything else. And maybe he'll learn to socialize like a normal person."

"That's mean," I swatted his chest again. "He's not abnormal, just different."

"Mean is my middle name, sugar." He leaned in, grinning, catching my lower lip in his teeth.

"Oh yeah?" I giggled, pulling back. "Mine's Diaz. I took my dad's last name as my middle name and my mom's surname. A lot of women were doing it as a small protest at the time, giving kids their maiden names instead of their husband's names."

Reaper was silent as I blabbered, and I realized the moment got serious.

"I don't actually have a middle name," he confessed. "My family thought they were useless and outdated. But," he sucked in a breath, "my real name is Rory."

A huge grin threatened to split my face in half. "*Rory?*"

"I know, it's dumb."

"It's not!" I cupped the sides of his neck, the giggles spilling out of me. "It's *so* cute."

"Shut up, woman. You trying to take my man-card away?" But he was smiling and tickling my sides, making me laugh harder.

I leaned into him, holding his face and laughing as I kissed him.

It was a good day and I was happy. I saw my friend, did my job that I loved, then came home to a man who cared about me. In that moment, life felt so simple and pure. The words tumbled out of me before I could stop them.

"I love you, Rory."

TWENTY-FIVE

REAPER

"I love you, sugar."

The words came out a hushed murmur against her spine as I kissed her there, tracing her beautiful back with my mouth.

"I love you." I said it between her shoulder blades that time and would say it over every inch of her body if she let me.

I never said those words to anyone, except to my parents as a child. I didn't even say it to Daren before he died. I was too busy being pissed off at him for giving me all of the vaccine while he wasted away.

He died never knowing how much I appreciated his wisdom, despite being younger than me. He thought I was pissed about him lying to me when I was honestly scared to death about going on without him. I should have told him it was okay, that I had this shit in the bag. I should have been a big brother to him, not a pissed off president. Because I could never imagine how scared he must have been to feel himself slowly slipping away.

Telling Mariposa I loved her didn't make up for never telling Daren, but I didn't want to make the same mistake again—waiting until it was too late.

Now those three simple words sent my pulse racing every time they left my mouth. It was a better adrenaline hit than riding. And I could have it every time I looked at my woman.

"I love you," I said with a kiss to the nape of her neck.

Mari moaned softly in her sleep, rolling onto her stomach. Fuck me, how could anyone be so perfect?

Her skin and hair contrasted breathtakingly with my white sheets. She looked like an angel sleeping on clouds. How ironic for her to be in the bed of a Demon.

Not to mention falling in love with one.

When she told me that in my study last night, I didn't even care that she used my real name. I knew she meant it.

And I said it back to her. Again and again. It was the last thing on my lips when I fell asleep and the first thing when I woke up.

"Damn," I breathed, just staring at her. "I love you, Mariposa."

"I love you, too..." she mumbled face down in the pillow, "...*Rory*."

"Goddamn it, woman!"

I yanked the pillow out from under her head and smacked her with it.

"I'm still sleeping, asshole!" Her legs kicked out, narrowly missing my junk.

"Liar," I cackled, rolling her over and pinning her

beneath me. "And I'd rather be Asshole than fucking Rory."

"I don't know why you hate it so much." She lifted her chin at me defiantly and it was fucking adorable.

"Because it's a stupid dipshit name."

"I think it's cute!"

"I," I grabbed her wrists and pressed them into the mattress on either side of her head, "am not *cute*."

Her smile was stunningly beautiful and devilish in a way that got me hard in an instant.

"Sorry to break the news, but you're actually pretty cute." Her head lifted to kiss my nose. "But I'll call you Reaper if it makes you feel like a badass."

"Woman," I sighed, lying my head down on her pillowy breasts. "You're enjoying this, aren't you? Pushing my buttons knowing full well I won't do anything about it because I'm fucking crazy about you."

"Maybe a little." Her hands smoothed down my back. "Okay, more than a little. But it's payback for you being a dick before."

I lifted my head to look at her, my expression now serious. "I deserve it, then."

"Yeah, you do," she tapped her finger against my lips, the devilish spark still in her eyes, *"Rory."*

I groaned and rolled my eyes but otherwise didn't complain.

"You believe me, right?" I caught her hand and kissed her fingers. "That I'm going to be better for you. I've never been in love before but fuck, Mari, I want to do this right."

"Reaper." She whispered my *true* name, running her

fingers through my hair. "I wouldn't be here if I didn't believe you."

I lowered my head back down to her chest with a sigh, still careful not to crush her under my weight. "I'm dreaming."

"Why do you say that?" she laughed, scratching lightly over my neck.

"I'm in love with a woman who loves me back. That kind of shit just doesn't happen to me."

"Should I call you Rory a few more times?" she joked.

"Call me that all you want. I'll just fuck you until you lose your voice." I kissed her collarbone. "Anyway, I still have all this club bullshit to bring me back to reality. Speaking of," I lifted my head up and gave her a long, languid kiss, "I gotta hold church, sugar."

"Okay, I'll be in the medic's office. Send anyone down who wants their injuries looked at."

"Will do." I kissed her again. God, why did she make it so hard to leave? "And thank you, beautiful, for looking after my people. I don't think I've told you that yet."

"Just doing my job, handsome," she smiled against my lips. "Oh! Before I forget," she grabbed my forearm, "I mentioned this to Jandro a while ago but I'd like to start vaccinating everyone. Kids especially. After the battle, I don't think having people donate blood would be a bad idea either. In case more serious injuries occur down the road. Can you bring those two ideas up to everyone?"

"You remember what I told you about my schooling, right?" I rolled to sit up at the edge of the bed.

"Don't act like you're not smart enough to relay a message." She nudged me with her foot. "I didn't even use any fancy medic words this time."

"No, but people might have questions I won't be able to answer."

"You can send them to me. I guess I should have office hours, huh?"

"You'll be repeating yourself a lot," I warned, sliding my pants up my legs before looking for a shirt.

"I already do that as part of my job."

"There's an easy solution to this, you know." The idea made me grin. It broke all the club rules but fuck if I cared.

She peered up at me curiously from the bed. "What's that?"

I leaned over and kissed her again, powerless to resist those lips.

"Come to church with me."

MARI FINALLY AGREED after some cajoling, but still had to stop by her medic's office first. Something about heartburn medication for Tessa.

In any case, it worked out because I had a hunch a certain man wouldn't have the balls to apologize to me with a woman in the room.

The conference room was empty when I arrived, save for Shadow.

"President," he stood from the table immediately. "May I have a word with you in private?"

"Certainly." I locked the door behind me then came around to the chair next to his. "Sit down, Shadow. What can I do for you?"

The big man didn't appear visibly nervous, but I knew this was difficult for him. Being alone helped, along with the fact that he trusted me almost as much as Jandro. Still, speaking didn't come naturally to him.

"I want to apologize for my actions the other day," he said. "I meant no disrespect to you or your woman."

"You can call her Mariposa," I said.

"Mariposa," he repeated softly, his fingers twitching in his lap for a moment. "On top of misunderstanding what she asked me, I didn't know she was yours. But Jandro explained it to me, and I know better for the future." His odd-colored gaze met mine straight on. "I promise you it won't happen again. I'm sorry, Reaper."

"Apology accepted." I clapped him on the arm. "You're a good man, Shadow. I know you didn't mean anything by it and I'm glad you're able to learn from this."

He nodded, now looking visibly more nervous. "I still have to apologize to her—Mariposa—directly."

"You shouldn't have any issue with that." I got up to unlock and open the door. "I think you'll find her forgiving."

"Women are not forgiving in my experience," he muttered.

"To be fair, Shadow," I sighed, rounding the table to

my seat again, "your experience is the exception, not the norm."

"That is what everyone tells me," he said. "But I have nothing else to compare it to."

"You will one day," I assured him. "Maybe even with Mari's help."

He looked at me with a puzzled expression. "How?"

"No idea," I shrugged. "But she's smart. And she's kind. She only ever wants to help people." *And be an adorable pain in my ass by calling me Rory.*

"Those are good qualities."

"They are," I agreed. "If there's a way to help your...condition, I'm sure she'll find it."

"She won't want to help me," Shadow grumbled.

"You might be surprised."

The club started filing into the room and for a moment I was proud to see a room full of Steel Demons again, instead of only the usual faces from the road. But the thought of someone in this room betraying us, putting us in danger, quickly soured my mood and made my blood boil.

I smacked the gavel on the table the moment the room filled up and the door closed. All murmurings died down to hushed silence.

"I'll get straight to the point," I said. "General Tash betrayed us and has tried to take us out twice now, thanks to insider information. And one of you is the general's little bitch."

I allowed a pause to let that sink in. Everyone kept their eyes straight on me, no side-eyes to the man next to him.

"One of you," I went on, letting my eyes linger on every single man in the room, "has desecrated the Steel Demons patch. Every time you put it on, you do so under false pretenses. You're not loyal and you're a dishonest piece of shit. I have no room for the likes of you in my club. And when I find out who you are," I couldn't resist the cruel smile spreading across my face. "I'll feed your balls to my dog. And I'll make you watch."

At my side, Hades barked and licked his lips. I never trained him to respond to anything I said. He just seemed to know how to add dramatic effect to my threats. Whoever the weasel was just had to be squirming now.

"To the rest of you, the *true* Steel Demons," I stroked Hades' head, "Jandro told me how quickly you all came to our aid on the dirt bikes, assisted Mariposa with the wounded, and cleaned up the wreckage outside. You did me and the patch proud."

"We deserve a party," Jandro cupped his hands around his mouth like a megaphone, earning laughs and murmurs of agreement from the others.

"Fine, handle it." I waved a hand at him. "I assume we have steaks and charcoal leftover from last time. Actually, that brings up another point of business."

The murmurs died down again for me to speak. "Our business with General Tash has obviously ended," I said. "As he was the biggest trade partner we had, Gunner is out securing new trade deals as we speak. We are well-stocked for the time being, but there may be a transition period where we'll have to ration goods."

"In addition," Jandro jumped in after a nod from

me, "we have a surplus of firearms and other weapons from the Sandia outpost's armory which we fully intend to use. Once we eliminate Tash's bitch, we'll reach out to the MCs we're allied with and pool resources." He drummed his hands on the table. "We're going to war, fellas."

The whole room fell into stunned silence.

"Uh," Big G lazily raised a hand. "Which MCs are we allied with?"

"Iron Soldiers, Phantom Kings, and Dark Brother-hood, to name a few," I answered. "Gunner has his contacts, I have a few of my own."

A gentle knock came to the door.

"Ah, perfect timing." I stood from my seat and went for the door while everyone looked bewildered.

Hades trotted happily beside me, knowing exactly who it was. If we hadn't thrown anyone for a loop yet, a woman in church was certainly about to.

TWENTY-SIX

MARIPOSA

R eaper opened the door with a sly grin, a sign he was up to something. I just couldn't be sure what.

"Hey, sugar," he greeted me, low and husky. "Come on in."

No less than fifteen pairs of eyes stared at me as I followed him to the head of the table. And none looked more terrified of my female presence than Shadow.

Jandro just smirked and winked at me. He had to be in on the same joke as Reaper.

"This is Mariposa, if you haven't met her already," Reaper's hand skimmed along my lower back, a clear sign of possessiveness. "She's the club medic and wanted to implement some new things for our health. Go ahead, Mari." He leaned against the back wall and folded his arms, giving me the proverbial spotlight.

"Uh hi, everyone," I said uneasily. "So the first thing I would like to introduce is regular vaccinations, especially for children. Many diseases have been on the rise since the Collapse, most of which are preventable with a vaccine. It'll be the best thing for your immune system if you go out and possibly encounter a disease while on a ride."

"How do you take a vaccine?" someone asked.

"With an injection," I answered. "Sometimes a series of injections over several months, depending on the type of vaccination."

"What if you're scared of needles?"

"You have twice as many tattoos as anyone, Python, shut the fuck up," Jandro yelled across the room. "Go on, Mari. Ignore them."

"The second thing I would like to introduce is blood donations," I said. "I would like to keep stock of the four main blood types in case someone is so badly injured that they'll need a transfusion." I raised a hand. "This is all on a volunteer basis, of course. If you don't want to get vaccinated or donate blood, no one will force you. But the vaccines will only help you, and giving blood can mean the difference between life and death for you or your fellow Demons."

I swallowed the dry lump in my throat. "Any questions?"

"Where do we sign up?" Jandro grinned up at me from the table.

I couldn't help but smile back. "Anyone interested can meet me in my office. I can get you on a vaccination schedule and determine blood types with a simple test. Once I have a catalog of volunteers' blood types, I'll start taking donations."

A bunch of blank stares met my eyes and I swallowed another dry lump of unease. Had I completely gone over everyone's heads? Or were they still stuck on the fact that a woman entered their sacred club meeting?

Reaper came up behind me and gave my shoulder a reassuring squeeze.

"I'll be the first to volunteer." To everyone else, "Mari worked tirelessly all night to patch us up from the attack. You can trust her, not only with your own lives but your children's."

"Any medical issues you come to me with will also be kept confidential," I added. "This is something I take very seriously, so please don't suffer in silence because you're ashamed or embarrassed. Trust me, I've seen every body part and organ you can imagine, and probably some that you can't."

That got a chuckle out of some people.

"So please," I reiterated, "come see me if you're having any medical issues or just have questions."

Jandro raised his hand next. "I also volunteer for vacs and blood donation." He shot me a grin. "As long as you don't hurt me too badly."

"I won't if you won't," I retorted without thinking.

Chuckling, his eyes dropped to the table.

Reaper's hand on my shoulder moved to the nape of my neck.

"Thanks, sugar." The pet name and the contact on my skin seemed to send a clear message without explicitly saying it.

I was his. And I liked that a lot more than I thought I would.

"Thanks, everyone." I gave a small wave as I headed for the door. "You know where to find me."

———

"YOU OKAY WITH THIS?" Reaper's green eyes shone like bright jewels under my office lights.

"Of course. What matters is *you're* okay with it. You're the patient."

I glanced up at the dozen or so people crowded around my tiny office. Tessa was there, along with her two kids. So was Noelle, staring nervously at my blood-draw syringe despite the lengths of colorful tattoos decorating her arms.

"I want them to see that this isn't a big deal," Reaper said, lifting his eyes to our visitors. "That we don't have to be afraid of blood or needles or any of that shit. This can help us live longer, and therefore make the Steel Demons even stronger." He nodded at me. "Do what you gotta do, sugar."

"All right, I need your arm."

He extended his hand to me. I pushed his sleeve up past his elbow and placed the back of his forearm on the small pull-out table between us. Tying a strip of gauze around the widest part of his forearm, I began tapping the inside of his elbow in search of a vein.

"Why do you do that?" Tessa's older boy asked.

"This is to slow his blood-flow a little bit," I said, tugging on the gauze strip. "It helps me find a vein to draw blood from." Reaper's veins were already swelling inside his elbow. "Now," I said. "Here's a little poke."

I inserted the needle and opened the tube, then taped the needle down. A few people let out soft gasps as dark red blood flowed out of his arm and into the bag.

"That's all it is," I said, turning to everyone. "A pint of blood can potentially save three lives and it'll only take about ten minutes." I turned back to Reaper. "How bad was that?"

"Not bad at all," he grinned, staring at the needle in his arm. "Kind of a rush, actually."

"I want to go next!" Tessa's boy declared.

"Hey, little man," I rolled my stool over to him. "You're big and strong, but you need all your blood to grow even bigger right now. In a few years, though, you'll have some extra you can give if your mom says it's okay."

"Are there any, uh, side effects?" Noelle asked nervously.

"You might feel a bit weak and dizzy after donating. It's important that you don't exert yourself for several hours afterward. Drink plenty of fluids and eat well to help replenish what you donated. You might also feel sore and have a bit of bruising at the injection site but that will fade after a few days."

When that answer seemed to reassure her, I looked at everyone else. "Any other questions?"

Once Reaper finished up, the response was over-whelming. A line formed outside my office door of people wanting to donate blood, get vaccinated, talk to me about check-ups, or all of the above. I did my best to give everyone my undivided attention while also trying not to panic at the line growing longer.

But no one seemed to mind waiting. If anything, the hallway buzzed with excitement. And still, people kept a distance outside my office door to provide privacy to those I was seeing. It ended up being a long day, but one I'd been dreaming of for years. Seeing patients, putting fears to rest, and providing them with insight about their health and bodies. It was all I ever wanted to do with my life, and the Steel Demons MC made it happen for me.

When the last patient left, a tall, handsome man leaned into my doorway. He already had his arm bandaged so I jokingly made a shooing motion at him.

"Get out of here. I already saw you."

"No one told you I get extra benefits with the medic?" Reaper smirked, stalking toward me. "What did you think? Good turnout?"

"Yeah, really good. Amazing, even." I ran my hands through my hair and blew out a breath. "Now I'm dying to wind down with a drink and foot rub."

"I was hoping you'd say that." His arm hooked around my waist, drawing me against him for a deep kiss. "Let's go home, sugar."

MARIPOSA

"What's this?" I gasped in shock. "You're bringing me a drink?"

"Don't get too excited," Reaper smiled in spite of his grumbling. "We're still in the honeymoon phase."

He handed me a glass of wine, then moved my legs so I could extend them across his lap.

"Then I'll enjoy it while it lasts," I sighed in utter bliss, swirling the wine while his thumbs pressed into the arch of my foot.

"I'll make sure you do." His voice rumbled like a purr as his hands worked magic into my sore feet. "Did Shadow apologize to you?"

"No, not yet." I smacked my lips lightly with a sip of wine.

Reaper grunted out a sound of displeasure while gently squeezing around my ankle. "He needs to get on that shit."

"He's uncomfortable around crowds, right? All the people in my office must have made him nervous." I took another delicate sip. "Getting an apology is not even a big deal to me. As long as it doesn't happen again and it truly *was* a misunderstanding—"

"It's a big deal to me," Reaper snarled. "The apology itself and the principal of the matter. He cannot set the precedent of treating club women like whores, nor can he disobey a direct order from me. If he doesn't come to you tomorrow, I'll have to expand on his punishment for disobedience." His gaze softened as it traveled up the length of my legs. "You don't seem too upset by what he did anymore."

"I think talking to you right after, and having some time after the initial shock wore off," I swallowed another sip of wine, "I realized there was nothing really traumatic or awful about it. He didn't hurt me or coerce me, really. I didn't ruin things with you. It's in the past now and I'm at peace with it."

"So you *did* enjoy it then," he teased. "Shadow got a nice, fat cock for ya?"

"Might I remind you that my feet are *very* close to your balls, Rory."

"And they'll be curling in ecstasy before you're done with that wine, sugar lips." His fingers trailed up my calves with a devilish grin.

"Something I wanted to ask you," I gave my liquid courage another swirl, "what rule did I break? You mentioned it in the bath that night."

Reaper's hands rested on my shins as his head leaned back on the couch with a soft sigh.

"Sharing partners is taken very seriously in the culture I grew up in," he explained. "It's almost on par with moving in together, or even engagement in broader society. Outsiders thought we were total hedonists, addicted to sex and fucking anyone we looked at. But that couldn't be further from the truth."

"It was a relationship," I said. "A serious one, just with more than two people."

"Exactly," he nodded. "Our tradition was that the man would suggest another person to bring into the love life and eventually, bedroom. Usually it was someone the couple already knew and trusted."

"A mutual friend," I realized.

"Yes. Doing this was a sign that he trusted and loved his woman so much, he felt she deserved the love of another person in addition to his. Another partner to support her emotionally when the first man had other obligations. Someone to please her sexually in ways the first could not, or just to double her pleasure in general." He smiled broadly at that.

"That is fascinating," I breathed. "Didn't the men get jealous?"

"Sure, at times. But here's where the rules come in." He lifted a finger to count off. "Each person in the primary couple had the right to veto other partners. So if a woman wasn't into her man's suggestions, she could reject them. Likewise if she started to like someone her man didn't approve of, he could forbid that person from entering the relationship."

"I see." My brain soaked up this information like a sponge. I had no idea societies like this even existed. "So because you didn't approve of Shadow..."

Reaper shrugged, placing his hands back on my legs.

"I never considered him for you, honestly. If he made you happy, I don't think I'd mind. That doesn't seem to be the case, though." He turned his head to the side, looking at me with sexy, hooded eyes. "That's all this is really about. Showing that I trust you and I want you to be happy."

I had to take a moment just to sink into that, to sink into *everything* he said. Was I happy? At that moment, holy hell yes. My life felt meaningful. I had a community with friends, patients, and this man sitting across from me who drove me nuts but I couldn't help but love and crave with every fiber of my being.

Was being with Reaper enough for me? Again, yes. I'd had monogamous relationships before and lived in a culture that put monogamy on a pedestal all my life. I was confident I *could* be exclusively with him and him alone. But was I intrigued and even a little tempted by this offer he put on the table? Also yes. It felt like he set Pandora's box in my lap and cracked the lid open for the tiniest peek. I wanted to see more of what was inside.

"So you *have* considered other partners for me?" I said.

"Thought of, yes," he said coyly. "It's entirely up to you to approve them, though."

"Who?"

"I think you know," he teased, running a hand up to my thigh.

"Jandro," I breathed. "And maybe Gunner?"

"Mm, lucky guesses." He nudged my legs apart to massage my thighs. "Is it something you'd like to try?"

"How—" My breath hitched, distracted by the firmness of his hands on my flesh and moving higher up my legs. "How would you, or we, I guess, go about asking them?"

"One at a time," he said, fingers circling into my leg muscles. "I think we should ask Jandro first. He'd be more open to it. If anything, I think he's been waiting for me to ask him. Then we'll see how you feel. You might decide two is enough or that you want me all to yourself after all."

"Okay. We ask and then what?" I suddenly felt like a teenager asking for dating advice—from my own boyfriend, nonetheless. "All three of us spend time together? Or just me and him?"

"Whatever your comfort level is," Reaper assured me. "If you want me around, I'm sure he'll understand. But if things go well, you two should spend time alone to get to know each other."

I set my wine glass down on the end table and leaned forward to wrap an arm around his shoulders.

"And you'll really be okay with that? Me going off with him and..."

His hands slid up to my waist, pulling me closer into his lap.

"If you come home to me all smiles with a post-sex glow, a dreamy look in your eyes, and your legs all wobbly," he paused with a grin as I smacked his chest, "then I know my woman is happy and well taken care of. How could I be bothered by that?" His lips brushed my cheek until he reached my ear. "And if I feel you scream with my cock down your throat because another man is fucking you so good, you can't stop coming? Oh sugar, that'll be the *best*."

"Turns you on, does it?" I nudged my leg against the bulge in his jeans, growing thicker by the second. "Bringing other people in."

"*You* turn me on." He let out a lustful growl, running his hands up to cup my breasts. "Your body gets me hard as a rock. The sounds you make drive me insane. And I swear watching you come gets me so fucking high."

The last word barely left his mouth when I leaned in, dragging my lips across his in a needy plea.

He answered with a deep rumble of a moan in his chest, holding the back of my neck in place as our tongues lashed across each other as if fighting. His lips nipped and sucked at mine, making them so sensitive and pulsing. He moved my hand over his zipper, directing my strokes against his thick, solid length straining to be freed. After another deep, bruising kiss, he pulled away and gave me an order that made my core clench.

"Suck me."

A smile pulled at my lips. Sure, I'd do that. But my way. The Steel Demons president had no idea what was coming to him.

His breath hitched as I undid the button on his jeans and pulled down the zipper. Then my hand moved away, teasing the firm abdomen just above where he wanted me to focus. My fingers skimmed higher under his shirt, taking my time to trace the ridges of his stomach, ghosting over his nipples before flattening over the smooth planes of his chest.

His green eyes locked on me, he lifted his arms to peel the shirt off. Once it was gone, I feasted on his sexy tattooed skin with my eyes. This man was dangerous. Feared. Respected. And he was completely, utterly mine.

I began my descent back down his body—this time with my mouth.

He let out a delighted hum as I kissed the hollow of his throat, just between his collarbones, then dragged my lips lower to plant a kiss between his pecs. Never losing contact with his skin, I slowed way down when I reached his abs.

Now he let out a grunt of frustration, his hips shifting beneath me. I held back a smile, dragging my tongue over each defined muscle at a snail's pace.

"God, I love that tongue, sugar, but I need it on my dick." His voice was tight with restraint, his fingers curling in my hair to hold it away from my face.

"I know."

I sucked hard next to his hipbone, leaving him a nice little mark there. His cock was right under my face and I felt it twitch, begging for attention.

"Ugh, you are so bad," he groaned.

I kissed my way to his opposite hip, leaving a mark on that side, too, before peeling his jeans and boxers down to reveal him, fully engorged and absolutely mouthwatering.

"Ohhh fuck," he hissed when my tongue swirled the flared head.

I wrapped my hand around the base as my lips

sealed over the crown of his dick. His curses grew louder and more drawn out as I steadily took more of him into my mouth.

But it seemed he had sneaky plans of his own.

He caressed my neck and back as I leaned across his lap. A shudder passed through me as he groped my ass, then his fingers moved lower to the back of my thighs. For a moment, he just teased the skin just under my cotton lounge shorts. When his fingers moved to rub teasing circles between my legs, I released a moan around his shaft.

"Yes, beautiful, tell me how much you like this," he rasped, stroking me through the thin fabric.

I sucked him harder, shuddering with each swipe of pressure he applied to my clit. He waited until I made a slobbery mess of his cock before pulling my panties and shorts aside to touch me directly.

"Mm, you're soaked." His hand pulled away for one tortuous second and I heard him suck his fingers before touching me again. "Wouldn't you like another cock to fill you up while you suck me so good like that?"

I moaned the loudest I had yet, not only because his words were so filthy and hot, but he chose then to dip two fingers inside me. The feeling mimicked another man penetrating me and I found myself bucking against his hand, pressing back to take more, deeper.

"Greedy girl. You really do want two cocks, don't you?" He added a third finger, stretching me to my limit. "You want a nice big one pounding you while you please me with that tongue?"

I already started convulsing around him, but his

thumb on my clit did me in. I came hard, spasming around his fingers while I screamed around his cock.

I barely recovered when he pulled my head up, withdrew his fingers from me and pulled me roughly into a straddle position on his lap. He lifted me with an iron grip on my waist and pressed me down in one fluid motion onto his thick, rigid length already well lubricated in my saliva.

"So fucking good," he grunted out, arms around my waist as he drove up into me. "So fucking perfect," he added with a rough kiss to my neck.

I was on top but the control was all his. All I could do was hold onto his shoulders as his hips drove up like pistons, filling me up again and again until we both came undone with shudders and moans. He stayed seated inside me, fingers curled into my waist and face buried in my neck, until our rapid heartbeats slowed.

"At the party tomorrow night," he panted with a kiss to my forehead. "We'll ask Jandro then."

TWENTY-EIGHT

SHADOW

"**W**here you been, man?"

I closed my eyes, counting Jandro's steps across the grass as he approached me. Twelve. I was right again.

"I've been here."

I couldn't see his expression but I knew how he was looking at me—with one eyebrow raised. He liked to do that a lot.

"You've already worked out today, dude. You're just avoiding the inevitable."

I opened my eyes and turned to him, dropping the barbell I was using to stretch.

"Come with me?" I asked. "I could talk to Reaper alone, but with her..."

"Mariposa."

"With Mariposa, I—what if *she* doesn't want to be alone with me and I'll just make it worse?"

"Ugh, fine," he sighed. "I only have floor-to-ceiling's worth of fucked up bikes to fix and part out, plus I gotta get the patio ready for the party tonight, but I *guess* I can hold your hand while you talk to a girl."

I stared at him, puzzled. "Why would you hold my hand?"

"I didn't mean literally, it's an expression. Anyway, you coming to the party?"

"No, I don't think so."

"Why not?" He tossed out a handful of grain to the chickens, who came running over to peck at the ground where it landed. "You had a good time at the last one, didn't you?"

"I did, but I have a drawing I want to finish."

"Oh, that's cool. A drawing of what?"

"Just something I saw in the desert while we were on the road."

Jandro nodded without saying any more. I knew other people would press for more information and I appreciated that he didn't. He often annoyed me with how much he pushed me to be social, but I knew he meant well by it. He at least respected what I preferred to keep private.

"Shall we go to the medic's office?" he extended an arm to our home's gate leading out to the street.

"I suppose," I grunted, pulling my shirt back on and loosening my hair from its tie.

"Man, you're gonna get this over with," Jandro said as he led us out, "then afterward, you're gonna wonder why you were so worried in the first place. She's easy to talk to, trust me."

"No one is easy for me to talk to," I muttered. "Except you."

"Because I'm basically your dad, even though we're the same age."

I didn't know how old I truly was. My birth was never documented or recorded. I had barely any sense of time growing up, except from what the others told me before they disappeared. When I was taken to Jandro's prison, I didn't have ID or even a name to give them. I stood silently in the corner during intake, a full foot taller than everyone, so they called me Shadow. The prison dentist looked at my teeth and estimated my age to be between twenty and twenty-three. Jandro was twenty-one when we met, so he said we could share the same age.

Back then, I never would have imagined I'd walk freely in the daylight next to someone I considered a friend—nor eat big, filling meals every day and learn to ride a motorcycle. Sometimes I still wondered if my life in the Steel Demons was a dream, and my nightmares were my real life.

My hands started to shake as we got closer to the clubhouse, where the medic's office was. I couldn't tell if it was because I needed a drink or my anxiety about this whole situation. Probably both.

"You good, dude?" Jandro asked.

"No. But you're not going to let me walk away from this."

"Damn straight," he said. "Least of all because it's an order from your president, who will have both of our balls if you don't follow through."

"And most of all?" I grumbled.

"Because it's the right thing to do." He pulled open a door and led me in. "Her office is this way."

My feet dragged over the floor like moving through concrete. I balled my hands into fists in an attempt to stop the shaking. A sign sticking out above the door ahead said MEDIC with a square red cross. And the door was already open, fuck.

"Hey, Mari." Jandro's voice took on a different tone, the one he most often adopted when talking to women, as he leaned against the doorway and smiled into the room.

"Hey, Jandro! What brings you here?" came the cheerful, feminine voice from inside.

"I'm just chaperoning," he smirked, looking at me before jerking his chin toward the inside of the small office.

Shit. I really had to do this now.

My feet dragged forward until I reached the opening of the doorway and turned to face the last person I wanted to see.

She sat on a stool with wheels on it, brown hair piled on her head in a bun with a few wisps falling out. Her face no longer wore the pinched tiredness from the night she was healing everyone. Instead, her eyes were bright and she smiled easily. Even when I blocked her view of Jandro.

"Hi, Shadow," Mariposa greeted me. "What can I do for you today?"

My mouth opened but words refused to work. It felt reminiscent of coming out of my longest isolation period, when I hadn't spoken to anyone for about six months.

"I, um..." I cleared my throat, my gaze darting around the room for something to remind me of what I was supposed to say. "I would like to donate blood."

Fuck. No, that was wrong. But it was the first thing that popped into my head because she mentioned it at church yesterday.

"Okay, sure." Her smile widened at me as she gestured to another stool like the one she was sitting on in front of a small, pull-out table. "You can have a seat right there, and I'll walk you through it."

I looked back at Jandro and he lifted up a shoulder. His face looked like he was trying not to laugh.

Mariposa prepared some things on the main counter where she sat, while I maneuvered to where she directed me. The stool was far too small and low to the ground for me, and the table felt like it would break in half if I leaned on it too hard. So I stayed upright, trying to balance like a cartoon elephant on a beach ball that I saw on a television once.

"I won't keep you too long, promise," Mariposa said as she wheeled over to sit across the table from me. "First, I'd like to determine your blood type. I just need a drop of blood from your finger, and my test kit will tell me in about three minutes. Then the donation process will take about ten minutes. Sound good?"

I nodded. Thirteen minutes. I would definitely live for the next thirteen minutes.

Jandro was right. This wasn't as terrible as I thought it would be. But I still hadn't said what I came to say.

"Okay. Can I take your hand, please?"

I extended one arm across the table toward her, where she took my palm and turned it face up. Her gloved hands were so small compared to mine.

A memory flashed of her bare palms splayed across my chest. They looked so small then, too, and moved over my skin like they didn't want to leave any part of my torso untouched. It felt so nice and different. I wanted to touch her in return but couldn't bring myself to. None of the women before responded well to my attempts.

She's not like them, I reminded myself. Jandro made that very clear. She was Reaper's and therefore off-limits. I made a mistake and she was too frightened to do anything but go along with what I started. Even now, as she pressed something down over my fingertip and pulled it away, she was probably filled with fear. Some women hid it better than others.

"All right, just a couple minutes for the antigen markers to show up." She placed something on the counter and grabbed a small wad of cotton to press over my fingertip.

Holding it there with one hand, she grabbed a band-aid with the other. When she pulled the cotton away, a small drop of blood was on it. She swiftly wrapped the band-aid around my finger and wheeled a few feet away to her testing kit on the counter.

I sucked in a deep breath. It was now or never.

"I'm actually here because I owe you an apology."

She looked up at me with an expression I couldn't read, so I made sure to continue on.

"I'm not around people very much and there are some things I still don't understand." The words tumbled out now. It was slightly easier with my eyes glued to the band-aid on my finger. "I misunderstood what you asked me the other night. If I had known, I wouldn't have...done that."

She didn't say anything so I dared to glance up. Her eyes, a shifting greenish brown color like Jandro's, met mine directly. There was no fear in them. Not even the most stoic of men could fake that.

"It was wrong of me and it won't happen again," I said. "I'm sorry for upsetting you and not knowing my place."

Mariposa's hands folded in her lap and a small smile returned to her face.

"I accept your apology, Shadow. There are a lot of things I don't understand either, especially about life in an MC." Her head tilted to one side as she lifted one shoulder in a shrug. "Who knows? Maybe we can be friends."

I blinked as a small jolt of panic hit me.

"I've never been friends with a woman before."

"Well, we're going to see each other around a lot," she answered. "It would be easiest if we got along, right?"

"I guess so."

Her smile grew. The more she did that, the more I realized how pleasing it was to look at.

"I won't be all up in your business, but don't be too surprised at me saying good morning or hello to you."

She wheeled back to the counter and picked up her

test kit. "Huh, that's interesting. Your blood type is AB+. That's pretty rare."

"What does that mean?" I asked.

"Basically it means you can receive transfusions from any other blood type. However *your* blood can only be given to an AB+ person. So far, you're the only AB+ I've documented in the club."

"So my donation is not needed?"

"Donations are always needed. A matching blood type always works best in transfusion. If you'd still like to donate, you'd probably receive your own blood in the event that you needed it."

"Okay." I glanced up at the clock near her ceiling. It would keep me here longer than thirteen minutes. But now, I didn't mind that so much. "I'll still donate."

"Great! You can leave your arm right where it is." She wheeled a few feet away and pulled open a drawer to gather some things.

I looked over my shoulder once again, surprised that Jandro hadn't chimed in with his usual quips during our conversation.

Son of a bitch. He was gone.

I turned back just as Mari wheeled back over to me.

"I'm going to tie this here," her gloved fingertips skimmed over my forearm to loop a piece of fabric around it, "let me know if it's too tight."

She made no mention of my scars, nor did she pay them any particular attention. As she gently poked the inside of my elbow, I fought the nagging want to feel contact without the barrier of her gloves. I'd never feel anything remotely like her bare hands on me again, so I just had to accept it.

"You're going to feel a little poke," she murmured before piercing my skin with the needle. Of course, I felt nothing but the pressure of it and the sensation of my skin breaking.

My blood flowed through the tube and into the attached bag. The liquid was dark, almost black, and I watched it pool and slowly fill the bag. I'd seen my blood leave my body many times, but never like this. And never for a reason that would possibly help me in the future.

Mariposa and I sat there together in silence. She didn't seem at all bothered by being alone with me. Jandro probably left the moment I sat down.

"You don't feel pain, do you?" she said after a few moments. "Physical pain, that is."

I looked up at her, surprised. "That's correct. Not many people have noticed."

"I had a hunch the other night when I sterilized your wound with vodka, stitched you up without anesthesia, and got no reaction."

"Yes." I shrugged one shoulder the way Jandro did sometimes. "I suppose I'm fortunate. A lot of men were suffering that night."

"I'll give you that," she leaned one arm on the counter. "But pain is important, too. It's a signal to the brain that something is very wrong in your body. You can push yourself past your limit without that signal to stop you."

"You're the medic, so I'm sure you are correct," I

answered. "But my inability to feel pain has only been an asset to the Steel Demons. It means nothing holds me back when performing my duties."

She smiled at me. I swore I received more smiles from a woman sitting here with her for the past ten minutes than I had in my whole life. Jandro was right. She was easy to talk to. And easy to look at.

"You're also correct," she said, checking my donation bag. "Neither of us have to be wrong, even if we see things differently. If you don't mind me asking," she paused, eyes flicking up to my face, "how long have you not been feeling pain, your whole life?"

"Since childhood." I paused to do a quick estimation in my head. "When I was around twelve, I think. I felt pain before then."

Her gaze dropped to the scars on my arms and anxiety tightened like a fist around my chest. I hoped she wouldn't ask. I didn't want to talk about it and I didn't want to scare her if she pressed. I didn't need that demon riding around on my shoulders today.

But all she said was, "Well, I don't blame you for being glad that you don't feel it anymore."

Her hands moved swiftly, like two small birds, as she closed off the tube and withdrew the needle from my vein. In the next moment, she pressed a small piece of gauze inside my elbow and wrapped a bandage around to hold it in place.

"Leave that on for a couple of hours and take it easy the rest of the day." She rose from her stool to clean up, and was still shorter than me sitting. "Make sure you eat enough and drink plenty of fluids, preferably not alcohol."

I watched her place my bag of blood in a small refrigerator then looked down at my arm. "That's it?"

"That's it, Shadow." She smiled at me again. "Easy, right?"

"Yes. That was not at all unpleasant."

She laughed lightly, a sweet sound I wouldn't mind hearing again. Nothing like the raucous sound out of some people's mouths that killed my ears.

"Stop by if you need anything," she gave a slight eye roll, "medically-related, as I'm sure you know."

"Yes, I know now."

She smiled in a way that made her eyes close slightly at the far corners as she gave me a small wave.

"See you around, Shadow."

"I'll see you, Mariposa."

GUNNER

I bore down harder on the accelerator, pushing my bike to its limit.

The wind whipped past me so fast, it felt like fingers clawing at my face. And I still wasn't going fast enough.

Horus nagged at the back of my brain just as I was leaving Uncle Jerry's. My consciousness slipped into his body just in time to see his talons dig into the neck of someone I didn't know.

The rider screamed, clutching at his neck as blood spurted out while trying to bat at my falcon with the other hand. Horus flew away, the rider's jugular already severed, and gave me a bird's-eye view of the mayhem.

There was Sheol, our home. And a battle waging just outside our gate.

Tash, you piece of shit motherfucker. Wait, where's Mariposa?

Horus flew over the battlefield, soaring high but showing me every detail. Shadow stood in his seat, firing two guns at bikers coming straight toward him. Reaper was on someone else's bike, not his own, Hades running alongside.

My worry spiked as the one person I was looking for didn't appear. All the bikes kicked up shit tons of dust and even with Horus's eyes, visibility was shit.

Come on, baby girl. Where are you?

There!

I didn't see her at first because Jandro sat her in front of him—smart man.

A shot hit him in the shoulder and he jerked forward. Mari went to put pressure on his wound and he yelled something at her, probably to keep her hands hidden.

That was two days ago. I'd been riding all day and night, stopping only for piss breaks and to refuel, but I was still too fucking far away.

I'd seen through Horus since then, and everyone seemed okay. But it was wrong for me to not be there. Especially after finding out where Uncle Jerry's true loyalties were—wherever he would benefit the most.

I thought I could play the family card on him, even though I didn't give a shit about it. He harped about it ever since I was a kid. *Take pride in your family name, Gunner. You're a Youngblood, one of the last truly powerful American families. No matter what happens, you'll always have your family.*

I always knew it was a crock of shit, but he harped on it so much I thought he actually believed it. But now I had to be the bearer of bad news to Reaper—my trump card got us a steaming pile of nothing.

The night grew darker and I switched on my headlight. Any minute now, I should be able to see the Steel Demons flag calling me home.

I wondered how much had changed in the time I'd been gone, if anything.

Who are you kidding, Gun? You're just wondering if Mari missed you. And if she still wants swim lessons.

My light picked up small bits of debris strewn in the sand, which I carefully swerved and maneuvered around. This must have been where the battle hit. The big pieces must have all been cleaned up, though, which probably meant plenty of work for Jandro.

The sky was turning deep purple and navy blue, allowing me to barely make out the black flag high above the gate. I felt more of a sense of comfort and longing for my home here among these "thugs" than I ever did at any of my family's mansions. This was my real home.

As I drove closer, I pulled out a rifle strapped to my back in preparation for the gate signal. But something caught my eye.

Around the side of the wall, I saw a figure with a motorcycle standing in the darkness alone.

Curious, I veered off in that direction. There was nothing around Sheol for miles, and no reason for anyone to be outside the gate by themselves. It was probably nothing, but my captain of the guard instincts kicked in and I followed the urge to investigate.

I drove up slowly. They'd hear my engine at any moment now, so it wasn't like I was sneaking up on anyone. As I got closer I saw another person, this one standing with their back to the wall, apparently talking to the person on the bike. It was too dark to make out faces, but my gut screamed at me that something was fishy.

"Oh shit," someone said.

The person against the wall took off running. The rider kicked off and started speeding away. I just chuckled at the sheer amateur bullshit of this.

Sure, it was dark. But I wasn't a weapons specialist for no goddamn reason.

I aimed at the rider first, lining my sight up with the center of his back. Dumbass didn't even have enough sense to zig-zag.

The first shot hit him and he went tumbling off the bike, which crashed right after he did. Another machine to part out for Jandro.

The rider was likely dead so I went for the runner next, aiming at his legs. It took two shots but I had him flat on the ground, moaning in pain in seconds. He wasn't going anywhere, so I checked on the rider first. Yep, dead as a doornail.

I didn't recognize his face. Kicking his body over onto its stomach, his back patch read Razor Wire MC. These fuckers again, the same club that attacked us outside our home. Their emblem was a Jesus figure with barbed wire around his forehead instead of a crown of thorns. Perhaps ironically, my bullet hole landed right between Christ's eyes.

Now to find out who the fuck was the sneaky weasel talking to him. I had a hunch I'd inadvertently found Tash's bitch. At least I'd have some good news to bring to Reaper if so.

Without the use of his legs, the guy tried crawling away on his forearms, but obviously didn't get very far.

"Aww, where you going?" I asked, delivering a kick to his ribs. "I just started having so much fun."

"Ah, God! Please…"

"Please what?"

"Please, don't tell them. I'll do anything…"

"Little late for that, bucko. Now let me see who's taking Razor Wire and Tash cock up the ass."

I grabbed his pant leg and dragged him back around toward the front gate.

"Yo, Dallas," I waved at the guard on duty. "Let me in."

"Captain Gunner! Good to see you and glad you made it back."

"Me, too, man. Me, too. Want to see who our traitor is?"

The sack of shit behind me moaned his protest as if his opinion mattered. "No, please! Just let me explain to Reaper…"

"Oh shit, is that what you're dragging?"

"Yeah, shine your light over here."

He clicked on a large flashlight and aimed where I stood just as I flipped the little bitch face up.

"You!" I cried in disbelief.

MARIPOSA

The clubhouse patio was livelier than the first party I attended. Something about a battle just outside your walls and coming to a near brush with death made a person that much more appreciative about celebrating life.

People started drinking before the steaks even hit the grill. Children chased each other around and even Hades joined in on the playing, while their parents sucked face and toasted to another night together.

The whole time, my stomach fluttered at the thought of seeing Jandro, what Reaper would say, and how his VP would respond. And once I got a spiked lemonade in me, I even dared to wonder where the night would end up.

"Relax, sugar." Reaper slid an arm around me from behind, smacking a kiss on my cheek. "Don't be nervous. Enjoy the party."

"I'm trying." My fingers laced with his around my hip. "I just don't want to mess anything up."

"You could never. Just go with what feels right." He gave my ear a playful nip. "Worst case scenario, you come home with only me."

"Hm, I like the way you put that." I smiled up at him, leaning back into his chest as I started to sway to an upbeat song playing from somewhere. "Where's the music coming from?"

"Check this out." He took my hand and led me across the patio. "Dallas collects these things. Isn't this nuts?"

Noelle and Larkan sat on the loveseat next to a black rectangular thing on one of the coffee tables, where the music was coming from. Or rather, she was sitting more *on* him. Good thing, Reaper was in too good of a mood to complain.

"Look at these, Mari." Noelle handed me a stack of flat, square plastic cases. "Our mom and dads used to play these bands all time."

"Wait a minute, you mean that's a," I sorted through the cases, which sure enough had round discs inside, "a CD player? A real one?"

"It has a radio and a cassette player, too. Dallas said he has a record player in his house but it's too valuable to bring outside," Larkan added.

"Why did the old folks have to have the best music, huh?" Reaper asked, taking the loveseat across from them and pulling me into his lap. He nuzzled my ear, crooning the song currently playing. "With me it's gonna be a good story to tell. Cash, grass, and ass on the highway to Hell."

"Hey, guys."

I looked up, my heart jumping into my throat at the voice.

"Jandro, have a seat."

Reaper scooted over to give his VP room to sit while subtly shifting me over in his lap—putting me in the middle.

"Where's Shadow?" I asked, noticing the large man usually with him was absent.

"He wasn't in a partying mood, just wanted to chill at home tonight."

"Is he *ever* in a partying mood?" Noelle muttered, flipping through more CD cases.

"Hey, he came out last time and helped me grill corn! That's a lot for him."

"Sugar?" Reaper shot me an intense look that told me exactly what he was asking.

"He apologized in my office this morning," I answered. "All's said and done. It's behind us now."

He visibly relaxed. "Good." His eyes flashed with mischief now as he looked at me over his beer, and I knew easily what else was on his mind.

"So, uh," I turned to Jandro, my nerves eating away at me. "How are the chickens?"

He nearly choked on his drink. "You say that like you haven't heard Foghorn crowing at the ass-crack of dawn every morning."

"I actually haven't."

"She sleeps like the dead," Reaper shook his head at me. "I don't know how."

"I was a war medic and traveled by bus everywhere! I learned to take hard catnaps whenever I could."

"A little less catnap and a little more vampire," Reaper teased.

Noelle and Larkan chose right then to take a dip in the pool, and I knew the inevitable was coming.

Reaper's hand slid across my back and my heart felt like it was going to break out of my chest. I knew his touch was an attempt at being calming, but it only made me hyperaware of what was about to happen.

"Jandro," he began. "There's something Mari and I would like to ask you."

His VP's hazel eyes slid over to me, then back to him. "Yes?" he asked, his tone and expression cool.

"We're wondering if you'd like to join our relationship," Reaper's hand closed around mine. "As a second partner to her."

Jandro's eyebrows lifted but his expression remained otherwise unchanged as his gaze returned to me. "This is something *you* want?"

I took Reaper's beer for a drink of courage and swallowed it down along with the knot in my throat.

"I really appreciate you in my life, Jandro." My voice shook with nerves and I took a steadying breath. "You've been there for me in times when he hasn't."

Reaper nodded his agreement and I found the strength to keep going.

"You've protected me and listened to me. You were literally my shield when we got ambushed and I don't take that lightly at all. I'm so grateful for you, and I think we have...something worth exploring." My final breath released like air out of a balloon. "This is completely new to me and I have no idea what I'm doing. But I have to admit I'm intrigued by this dynamic that Reaper's told me about, and as long as you're all happy, I'm willing to give it a try."

"Like I said before, sugar," Reaper pulled my attention back to him, "this is all about your comfort level and making *you* happy. You have the power here."

"And if you're confused, talk it out with either one of us," Jandro added before looking across me to his best friend. "I gather you've learned a few things about listening and not flying off the handle, Reap."

"I'm a work in progress but I'm trying," he answered with an affectionate glance to me.

"I've already seen a lot of improvement in Rory," I agreed.

Saying his real name combined with the venomous look he gave me broke all of the tension of the conversation. Jandro slid off the loveseat and onto the ground in peals of laughter and I couldn't help the giggles myself.

"Oh my God," Jandro gasped while clutching his stomach, "I'll say yes just to see your fucking face when she calls you that."

"Is this what I have to look forward to?" Reaper grumbled, draining his beer. "You two stooges laughing at my expense?"

"Yes," Jandro and I answered in unison and burst out laughing again.

"I take it all back."

"No takesies-backsies!" I smacked Reaper's forearm, coaxing the reluctant smile on his face that proved he was joking.

Somehow in our giggle fest, I found myself leaning closer to Jandro as he got back on the loveseat.

"So, what do you say?" I asked when the laughter died down and my nerves came fluttering back with a vengeance.

Jandro shot me a charming grin, reminiscent of when I first met him.

"I think you should come closer and find out, *Mariposita.*"

My first instinct was to look back at Reaper, to make sure this was okay with him, but I kept my gaze forward. I already knew how he felt, now I just had to figure it out for myself.

I leaned in and Jandro met me halfway.

The kiss was soft, only a peck at first like the rushed one he gave me at the start of the ambush. He paused, his breath a light tingle on my lips before I closed the distance again and opened up to him.

He met me for every beat, never taking the lead like Reaper, but just matching me with gentle exploration. His lips were pillowy soft and his tongue swiped across mine playfully, but never forcefully pushing into my mouth. Just like any other time with him, kissing Jandro was lighthearted and with no pressure.

When we paused for a breath, I felt a hand caress my nape. Reaper's hand.

I turned to him, not knowing what to expect on his face but he only smiled at me before giving me one of his signature, domineering kisses. A sharp thrill ran up my spine at the contrast between his mouth and

Jandro's, and maybe just from the sheer fact that I was kissing two men.

He released me for air and Jandro stroked my cheek, prompting me to turn to him where he awaited with a sly grin. This time, his tongue was more adventurous, his kisses deeper and more passionate but still with the same softness.

Reaper's hand kneaded my thigh as I kissed his vice president, his breath tickling my neck before leaving a bruising kiss on my shoulder.

Holy shit, this was intense.

My body didn't even feel solid anymore. I felt like I had to be melting down to the floor with how fired up these two men made me. And this was just kissing.

I broke away from Jandro, turning back to my green-eyed lover when a loud *pop* made me jump.

"Gunshot," Jandro said immediately, jumping to his feet.

"Where? Inside the gates?" Reaper growled, leaning over to reach underneath the couch.

"Guys, what's—"

Pop! Pop! Two more shots fired.

"Stay here, Mari." Reaper pulled two handguns out from under the couch and tossed one of them to Jandro.

"Better yet, go inside," Jandro told me. "Get all the women and kids inside."

The music stopped and the mood shifted from celebratory to tense in an instant. Men pulled weapons from all kinds of hidden places and ushered their women toward the clubhouse.

"Wait a minute," Reaper squinted toward the front gate entrance. "Is that Gunner?"

"Gunner?" I went to go see but Jandro blocked me with his arm.

"Hang on, let's figure out what's going on."

"Hah!" Reaper called out with a huge grin on his face and set his gun down. "Look what the birdman dragged in!"

Hades went running down the street toward the main gate with Horus flying right above him. Cheers erupted from the men now raising their weapons in the air as they crowded around to hug the man coming up to the clubhouse.

"A party in my honor? You shouldn't have," the blond demon laughed as he and Reaper clapped an arm around each other.

"Welcome home, brother," Reaper playfully messed up his hair. "What'd you bring me?"

"I brought you nothing but *this* was whispering to a Razor Wire right outside the gate when I pulled up."

I only then realized he'd been dragging a man behind him, who left a long trail of blood on the street all the way up to the clubhouse patio.

"Oh my God," I whispered, bringing my hands to my mouth. He'd been shot in each leg and would bleed out without medical attention soon.

"Python," Reaper spat the man's name with disdain. "What were you telling the Razor Wire, huh? Details from our church meeting?"

"Reap...please..."

"Where is the Razor Wire?" Jandro asked.

"Dead," Gunner reported. "Shot him in the back. Another bike for you to part out, bro."

"Great," Jandro mumbled. "More work."

Gunner's bright blue eyes focused on me for the first time and he shot me that dazzling smile I didn't realize I missed so much. "Hey, baby girl," he said softly.

"Hey, Gun," I returned.

"I asked you a question, you two-timing bag of shit!" Reaper grabbed the man's shirt and dragged him to the nearest fire pit. There he pushed Python's face next to the coals until he started screaming.

"The allies! I was telling him the other MCs we allied with and he was going to send it up to Tash. Reaper, I'm so sorry..."

"Well, even if Gunner wasn't the best shot on this side of the Mississippi," Reaper yanked him by the hair away from the fire. "You still would've been fucked, because I made those MC names up. I would've found you out sooner or later, you fucking bottom feeder. So congratulations, Python. You'll be the first to find out what happens to those who betray the Steel Demons."

"Reaper." I stepped forward, saying his name loudly to make sure I got his attention.

"Yes, Mari?" he gave me a curious look in return.

"Do you need him alive? For the next day or whenever you deal out his punishment?"

"Yes, maybe even for a week." The Steel Demons president lifted his chin at me. "Why?"

"He's losing a lot of blood and may die if he doesn't get a transfusion. I won't be nice but I'll heal him enough to keep him alive for your needs."

Reaper approached me slowly, a sinister smile growing on his face. Years ago, maybe even a week ago, I would have feared that smile. Only days ago, I feared what this man was capable of. What he may have done in the past and what he had yet to do in the future to protect his people.

But now his people included me, and I only burned with passion and love for the man cupping the nape of my neck, dragging his thumb across my cheekbone as his green eyes locked onto mine.

I was still a medic. I would always do my best to save lives and heal the broken. But I was no longer powerless in this broken down, collapsed society. I had people I loved, friends worth protecting, and nobody was going to hurt them without paying the consequences.

"That's my girl," Reaper said softly. "My Steel Demon girl."

Epilogue

REAPER

I watched the smoke from my cigarette drift into the night air and fade into nothing. The sky from my balcony was vast and speckled with stars.

One of the few times I paid attention in school was during an astronomy lesson. The teacher said every time we looked at stars, we were looking at thousands, maybe even millions of years into the past because light had to travel so far to reach our eyes.

Most of those stars had burnt out by now, or collapsed in on themselves to become black holes. I wondered if distant worlds faced rises and falls in their own societies like we had, and if they corrected their ways before their own suns died out.

Chaos and collapse wasn't uniquely human, I was sure. But right now it was peaceful. Tranquil, even.

Mari hooked Python up with fresh blood and stabilized him from Gunner's shots. She was worn out after that and wanted to come straight home. I let her, only after a long goodbye kiss from Jandro. Some people wanted to keep partying on the patio and they were free to. I thought about going back after Mari went to bed, but apparently I wanted to sit on the balcony and think about dying stars instead.

"Reaper."

I looked over my shoulder to see Noelle in her silk kimono, hugging her arms tightly around herself.

"What's up?"

My sister looked at me nervously. "I dreamed about him again."

I returned to facing forward with a sigh. "What do you want me to do about this, Noelle?"

"Stop acting like it doesn't mean anything, for one thing."

"It doesn't. It's just dreams. He was our brother and you miss him."

"Rory, you *know* they're not."

The cigarette paused on its way to my lips before I took a deep drag. Unlike my woman, Noelle did not call me by that name to tease me. I heard her slippered feet come up closer behind me.

"It's not just dreams," she repeated. "Daren is *talking* to me—"

"He's dead, Noelle."

"I know, but *something* about him isn't. You remember all that stuff he said—"

"A bunch of horse shit nonsense."

"That came true!"

She walked around to stand in front of me, blocking my view of dead stars.

"Tonight, he told me the love of your life would love

four men, and that you would lose her forever if you chose to kill one of them."

"Yeah, that sounds like common fucking sense to me, not a prophetic vision."

"He said I would only love one man for the rest of my life," she continued, biting her lip. "I think he was talking about Larkan."

"Fucking Christ, sis, you just met the guy! And what happened to him just being a stray?"

"He said something else, too, and that's what's bugging me the most."

"What?"

"That when we're called upon," her voice took on a harrowed tone, "we must obey the order."

"Called upon by who?"

Her eyes shifted to the sleeping dog lying next to me.

"The gods."

TO BE CONTINUED TO BE CONTINUED IN FEARLESS - BOOK 3 OF THE STEEL DEMONS MC SERIES.

CLICK HERE TO PRE-ORDER FEARLESS!

About the Author

Crystal Ash is a USA Today Bestselling Author from California. She loves writing steamy, heart-wrenching romance with tortured heroes, especially if they're in a reverse harem. Crystal's other loves include animals, mythology, and well-crafted alcohol, most of which can also be found in her stories.

When she's not writing, she's probably drinking craft beer with her husband or trying to coax her feral cat into accepting affection.

crystalashbooks.com

facebook.com/Crystal.Ash.Romance

instagram.com/crystalashbooks

amazon.com/author/crystalash

bookbub.com/profile/crystal-ash